DRIFTING
HOUSE

DRIFTING
HOUSE

KRYS LEE

faber and faber

First published in the US in 2012 by Viking Penguin,
a member of Penguin Group (USA) Inc
First published in UK in 2012
by Faber and Faber Ltd
Bloomsbury House
74–77 Great Russell Street
London WC1B 3DA

Printed and bound by CPI Group (UK) Ltd, Croydon, CR0 4YY

The right of Kyrs Lee to be identified as author of this work
has been asserted in accordance with Section 77 of the Copyright,
Designs and Patents Act 1988

A CIP record for this book
is available from the British Library

ISBN 978–0–571–27618–9

FSC
www.fsc.org
MIX
Paper from
responsible sources
FSC® C101712

2 4 6 8 10 9 7 5 3 1

To Amy, who knows

CONTENTS

There is a waving senatorial candidate with false teeth and hair implants in X, flooding in B, a famine in K, a civil war in R, the first democratic elections being held in S, an oil war raging in D, an actor as president presiding in Z, a nation splitting apart in T, a museum being constructed in L, a snowstorm devastating in U. And there is solar time, nautical time, inconsequential time, the time of memory, Greenwich Mean Time, geologic time, the drift of snow and sand and people, the cycle of whale sharks and spotted nutcrackers always returning home, their sense of time more instinctual than clocks or chronometers, and more exact.

DRIFTING
HOUSE

A TEMPORARY MARRIAGE

For three years after her ex-husband and their daughter, Yuri, disappeared to California, Mrs. Shin had designed clothes by day and sold handprinted scarves by night to save the necessary sum of money to depart Seoul and come to America. In order to find her daughter, she had assented to move into a stranger's two-bedroom condo on the fringes of Culver City—like two apartments! They would share the common space, nothing more. That had been the agreement.

But now that she had arrived, she saw that the living arrangements could be dangerous. The duplex was hot and cramped inside: a thready chintz sofa, the display cabinets heavy with souvenirs, the cumbersome oak table stained with the marks of sweating glasses, all seemed to touch one another. The kitchen faced the living room, and the living room, Mr. Rhee's bedroom. If he leaves the door open, she thought, we will see each other each time I look up from the cutting board. The lamp that Mr. Rhee switched on cast more shadows than light.

"Welcome to your new home." As Mr. Rhee spoke, his hands fluttered skittishly, batting at the air as if there were invisible mosquitoes. "Well, not really so new, but everything works well, well enough."

"Yes, it is a new home for me, isn't it?"

She did not want to look at him, understanding that she was aware of him as a man, and that gave him an immediate advantage over her. But she found herself looking. He was gangly and quick like a badminton player, unlike her ponderously built, strong ex-husband, and she disliked her disappointment. His doughy eyelids and sagging cheeks wore more sadness than she approved of, aging his face beyond his fifty years; his baggy peppermint-striped sweatpants smelled like a hospital gown and telegraphed his recent misfortunes. Even after the shame of her husband's departure five years ago, she had behaved like the fashion designer she was: she had never sanctioned mix-matching her bras and panties or privileged anyone to see her without an Hermès silk scarf, all efforts that gave her the appearance of confidence. Even after she lost her daughter, she had not allowed herself public displays of grief.

"I've left you the large room upstairs," he said. "I don't need a lot of space."

Mrs. Shin thanked him, all the time wondering if he was as innocuous as he looked.

"Well, shouldn't we document this—predicament?" she asked.

They needed photos to authenticate their engagement, then their marriage, to immigration.

"Predicament?" he said. "Well, yes, I suppose that's what it is."

She tolerated Mr. Rhee's arm around her shoulder, his parched white hair like the roots of spring onions, the dry-cleaning chemicals on his plaid shirt—a professional hazard of running Pearl Express, a dry-cleaning business. His garlicky breath scraped her nose. He, too, must have endured her stale travel smells.

After he set up his camera on the living room table, they both forced a smile until the timer clicked, the shutter snapped back, and she drew away. He continued to gaze.

She said into the silence, "Is there a rice grain on my nose?"

She had chosen not to marry some lonely Korean widower in America the old-fashioned picture bride way. The K-fiancée visa, and the next step, the marriage visa, had cost her a tidy sum precisely so he would not confuse this "predicament" with love.

"You have such young skin," he said, admiring her smooth, round face, her eyes the shape of plumped kidney beans.

She said, "I'm not looking for a real husband. I thought that was clear."

She was tired and frightened, so her words clicked like stilettos on tile.

She added, "I prefer a world without men."

"Don't worry," he said, blushing, twisting bunches of his hair with his hand. "I live for my boys. If you had children, you would know what I mean."

During Park Chung-hee's dictatorship nearly thirty years ago, Mr. Rhee had quit his engineering job at Hyundai Heavy Motors and immigrated to America with his wife. The family of four had settled in the basement of a kind American couple and cleaned office buildings until purchasing their own dry-cleaning store.

They had done well enough until the recent recession, which had even lawyers watching their expense accounts. Until Mr. Rhee's wife had abandoned him for an American man she met in salsa classes, he had watched Korean news clips of the developing country's daily disasters—student demonstrators attacked by pepper-spray bombs in 1986, the Sampoong Department Store collapse that killed generations of families in 1995—and convinced himself that he had been right to leave, even after the country flourished and began giving academic scholarships to the brightest from Guatemala to Mongolia, and setting trends in film and technology.

Mrs. Shin knew another Korea. In 1996 she had married up. A glittering four-hundred-guest Hyatt Hotel wedding, a Tiffany diamond flashing on her finger, and a villa nestled high in the hills, like a medieval castle overseeing the neon signs and pollution of Seoul, had transformed her. But money in Korea meant residing with the in-laws until the new bride was made acceptable; it meant surveillance and criticism. While hip-hop became the rage and women were sworn in as senators in the National Assembly, Mrs. Shin had subordinated herself to her husband's will, rivaled her mother-in-law for his affections, and accepted all blame when she remained childless the first six years of marriage. After nine years of a difficult, exciting life together, her husband had said that he could not do it anymore, that they were not healthy for each other, and left with their daughter. She was no different from Mr. Rhee; she felt that she had failed at living.

On that first night in America, Mrs. Shin's failures returned to her in her dreams. As she slept, her hands, those animals of habit, clutched at her crotch, a spot that she forbade herself to touch when awake. She dreamed of a missed appointment, a flippant remark, and the rituals of violence they would cause. Her husband lifted her by the slant of her black hair. His fist smashed her nose; his right foot bruised her ribs, her breasts. A purple flower bloomed across the ridge of her back, her hair fell out like dried leaves. She woke up trembling with excitement, her arms filmy with sweat and the residual scent of sex. She reached for her dressing gown in the dark and covered herself.

Downstairs she sat and sipped from a glass of water only after she spread a handkerchief on the sofa. The carpet roughened up by previous tenants and the desperate cheer of the coffee table's dusty plastic roses insulted her sense of propriety, so she started up, unwilling to sit any longer in the germ-infested room, when she heard a repetitive tapping. She could not bear not knowing, so she tiptoed over and cupped her ear to Mr. Rhee's door. To her horror, and delight, the door gave in and opened.

There he was, in ridiculous reindeer-patterned shorts and a shirt covered with tiny coconut trees. He stood behind a Ping-Pong table, the room's only substantial piece of furniture—if it could be called furniture. Across the table from him, a squat ball machine spat out a ball from one of the five mouths in its rotating head. The whip of his paddle shook the net as he chopped, covering the entire table with his forehand. He was more aggressive behind the net than the man she had determined him to be.

She laughed nervously. "Surprise," she said.

Mr. Rhee dashed to the robot and switched it off.

"Have visiting hours changed in 2011?" he said. "It must be past two in the morning."

He fanned himself with the paddle as he took in her billowing white gown and her cropped hair matted to her scalp like hairnetting.

He added, half-smiling, "I thought you liked your world without men."

His mouth was thin and stretched back. A line of sweat ran down toward his solar plexus. Her body became alert when she saw the bottle of rice wine that he had been drinking alone, and with head bowed, hands clasped behind her, she approached, aroused by the idea of this man out of control.

"A drink? Korea's finest," he said, balancing the cheap rice wine that Korean men favored on his head.

She nodded, suddenly thirsty.

He walked to an orange crate, his table, and poured her a thimble-size glass of the *soju*. She accepted the clear rice wine. She was so close she could see a vein in his neck throbbing, and she found herself wanting his dry lips, his hands tight around her neck. But when he kissed her, his lips were tame, disappointing. His hands stayed limply at his sides.

She turned so his second kiss missed her lips and descended on her cheek.

Immediately after, she patted her lips dry on her sleeve—she would wash before bed. He rubbed furiously at his hair, his eyes looked for somewhere to rest. Then he crawled underneath the Ping-Pong table and fumbled with the cotton *yo* that he now lay on top of, escaping into sleep.

"Sleep will do us good," she said decisively, and fled upstairs. She locked the door behind her.

The next morning Mrs. Shin disinfected the bathtub with a travel-size spray she always carried with her. She showered, dried her bob into two symmetrical points, and steam-pressed her white linen skirt suit, though she had nowhere to go. When she came downstairs, Mr. Rhee was preparing bean curd stew, dried yellow corvina, and small plates of cooked bracken and balloon flower roots. Mortified to see a man in a kitchen, she tried to wrench the spatula away, then she remembered last night's scene. This was America, she reasoned, as Mr. Rhee hugged the spatula. Hadn't she come to live differently?

Over breakfast they were careful and cordial to each other, their eyes converged on the bubbling *ttukbaegi* of stew.

"America's a dangerous place," Mr. Rhee warned her.

"I'm not afraid of danger," she said, unwilling to take advice from a man who slept under Ping-Pong tables.

He told her that to their right sat the Verdugo Mountains, and to their left, a shopping center the size of Seoul's Olympic Park with a Korean supermarket, video store, and salon specializing in Asian hair. And in a small building rented from the American Methodists was a Korean church, where the community's business deals were made. A Korean lawyer, a dentist, an optometrist, even a pet stylist, populated the mini-mall. Two cable stations broadcast Korean programs exclusively. She could, he reasoned, comfortably manage by confining herself to this one-mile area.

Mrs. Shin listened, nodded agreeably, and within a week purchased a burgundy-colored Hyundai Excel from a used-car lot.

Its back door didn't open, she had to hit the driver's window twice to roll it down, the left signal indicated right, and the right signal indicated left. She inched the car onto the highway toward Koreatown. Her broad forehead beaded with sweat as a truck the size of a small house whizzed by on a curving overpass and sent her car rolling on its axles, but she sang loudly to herself until her car stabilized. The sky outside the window was empty even of clouds, and the mountains were an unfamiliar, vast landscape of desert. She was not certain that Yuri still lived in California; she considered herself without a country. She couldn't afford to be scared.

Detective Pak was a lean silver-haired man in black slacks, white collar shirt, and wire-frame eyeglasses, an unadorned, efficient costume that matched his straight nose and blunt fingernails. His greeting was crisp and uninflected, unhurried and uninterested. He was a man who cared about details: handpainted bookmarks were stacked neatly at the edge of bookshelves crowded with books of poetry, a greenhouse of plants in descending sizes lined the small office, and, most worrying, an accounting exam certificate with his name, Gilho Pak, stenciled in, and a diploma from Korea's best university, Seoul National, were displayed in matching cedar frames behind him. She had hoped for a second generation with sloppy Korean, a man raised on hamburgers and fries, someone who might not have crossed the Pacific with his patriarchal ideas intact. Instead she got Detective Pak.

He shut her skinny file. "When you first called me, you claimed your daughter was kidnapped."

"But in a way, Dr. Pak, she was."

She always called people doctor when the situation required flattery.

He did not look flattered.

"If she's been kidnapped, I'm the last Joseon prince. I learned your husband got legal custody when you divorced." He gazed at her with a coolness she was unused to in men, and she wondered with amusement and worry if she, despite her efforts, now looked her age. He said, "And now you're remarried?"

So that was what he was thinking. That she was another Korean mother who had abandoned her daughter in order to remarry.

She looked for family photos on Dr. Pak's desk: for the young son and daughter, a svelte wife in golf shirt and shorts, but there was only a photo of Dr. Pak standing beside a young man with large, despondent eyes. Dr. Pak turned the photo over when he saw her looking. Still, she assumed he called his wife *jip-saram,* literally *houseperson.* Undoubtedly she made him two hot meals a day, the children would attend Ivy League schools, or at least UCLA or UC Berkeley. Nothing truly terrifying had ever happened to him, which gave her the small comfort of someone who had suffered. The vision of that excruciatingly ordinary life, that bonhomie, made her shudder. She wanted to want it; she loathed it.

He doodled question marks on letterhead stationery.

"It's a lovely family photo," she said.

"Samo-nim, why'd you let her go?" he said, his voice and gestures mechanically polite. "Do you know what it means, to lose your kids?"

She sat as erect as a queen. Then smiling, she said, "Dr. Pak, your job must be so emotionally taxing. I consider myself permanently bound to you."

"I need the real story." His gaze was unswerving in its need to understand. "So you gave up and agreed, and now you don't?"

"You're paid to be a detective, not a . . ." She struck the table with her purse. "You don't know what happened. Dangshin, you know nothing about me!"

He apologized, suddenly confused and upset in a way that made him more human, but she was too furious to stay. She marched out of the office. From the car, she watched pigeons snap at scraps of rotting pickled radish. The trunks of palm trees that she felt an urge to dress swayed precariously. She had lost face. Still, she would not share her secrets: how powerless she had been when her husband had bribed judges and taken Yuri away. How, on their last meeting, he had jammed a fat envelope of bank checks into her hand, saying, "You will start over." Or how she had refused the money that she needed, refused to retreat in the quietly disgraced way hundreds of divorced Korean women had, to one of the many Koreatowns in America. Only then the unexpected had happened. Within a year her husband and his lover had disappeared with Yuri.

She reknotted her scarf and jiggled her facial muscles loose with her knuckles. Look humbled, look wrong, she told herself, and turned back to his office.

She waited. Between Detective Pak's rare updates, Mrs. Shin fabricated a paperwork life for the marriage interview and adhered to a punishing productivity. She took brutal hour-long runs at five in the morning, then attacked the house with an artillery of vacuums, mops, and toothpicks; she negotiated an under-the-table sales job at a Koreatown boutique, which soon enjoyed a twenty percent sales increase. Twirling her ivory sun parasol above her head, she sought out strangers to practice English on, including Jehovah's Witnesses that Mr. Rhee said were "reliable company." She charged at her new life, but without hope, because hope was painful, dangerous.

As they amplified their story of marital bliss with new photographs, she learned that Mr. Rhee chewed green tea leaves to clean his teeth and that his nervous hand motions were usually practice swings for upcoming tournaments. That he donated extravagant sums he could not afford to the Los Angeles Mission, that he was intimidated by his English-speaking children attending East Coast universities. He was the retiring type but could not abide the abuse of women or children, which he said was as common as the flu in the immigrant community. Once, when Mr. Rhee stopped a man from spanking his child, the man smashed Mr. Rhee's eye and might have knocked out his teeth next if Mrs. Shin hadn't clubbed the man with her Bottega Veneta handbag. He was lonely and wanted her friendship, her company, and more, but she pretended not to notice.

One evening after work, she caught a random bus out of Koreatown, hungry to break up the routine of the days, and finally disembarked in an area called San Julian Park. It was the other America that had Mr. Rhee trembling, but she stepped off the bus so bored, she welcomed disaster. She strolled around the perimeter of the park, wanting the terrible to happen, but a trolling group of teenage boys merely stared at her and left her alone. A few homeless men crawled out of their cardboard tents and asked her for change, glue, anything you got, they said, their hands patiently held out for the token kindness they did not seem to expect. She tripped over a man with a Jesus beard lying on the grass, his blue eyes wasted, a bloody needle jammed into his emaciated thigh. Only one black boy on a tricycle briskly slapped her buttocks as he blitzed by, giving her a tiny thrill. But that was it.

She wandered until she saw a gas station phone booth lit by a dim streetlight. The foreign, starless sky oppressed her. A woman wearing only white sports socks and a torn trench coat limped across the street without looking left or right as if she no longer valued her life.

Mrs. Shin called after her, "Where am I?"

The woman cackled. "Don't you know?" And she went on.

She didn't know what else to do. She called Mr. Rhee.

"Pearl Express!" Mr. Rhee's foggy voice crackled. "How can I help you?"

"It's Mrs. Shin."

"Oh, yes, of course. I must have had a little nap—I have a mat, you see. *Saesang-heh!* It's nine-thirty! It's the Sealy mattress, a very comfortable mat."

Mr. Rhee would spring up from a creaky mattress with his nervous energy. The smells around him would be the clean, honest smells of chemicals and stale coffee grounds, and this comforted her somehow.

"Did you have rice?" she asked, which always meant, Did you eat?

"I had a sandwich," he said, and they both knew that this meant that he had not truly eaten.

"I'm somewhere near Julian Park—"

"Skid row! Where exactly was the accident?" There were the sounds of panicked preparation. "Don't move! I'll find you soon."

She said, "*Ani,* I'm safe, I think. It's just that—" She was mortified to find herself crying.

"Our poor Okja!" With genteel, outdated gallantry, he said her name for the first time. "*Saesang-heh!* What has befallen us?"

"Mr. Rhee." Her body sagged against the cold glass of the telephone booth. She laid her head against the sticky surface left by hundreds of hands, and into the receiver, she whispered, "I lost my daughter. Her name is Yuri."

Mr. Rhee insisted on visiting Detective Pak on his own, and by the week's end, Mrs. Shin consented. It was four months into her time in America. Friday after work, time dragged even more than usual while she cleaned. She scoured the immaculate kitchen and bathroom tiles; she furiously dusted the shelves sinking with books. She kept her eyes off the clock. While she polished the plaques that served as bookends, she noticed the engraved names: his name, Moonhyung Rhee, and underneath, Kyunghee Rhee. Doubles in the 1996 Koreatown League Championships. They moved her, those worthless monuments.

Now that the house shone like a trophy, there was nothing to distract her. She flipped through the movie channels, but make-believe stories did not interest her. She paced back and forth, clapping her hands together repeatedly to improve her circulation. Finally, after she had paced through all corners of the house available to her, she entered Mr. Rhee's bedroom. She strolled around the Ping-Pong table. Before bed he would place his eyeglasses on the wooden crate printed with FLORIDA ORANGES. In the fractured moonlight he would crawl under the table that he and his Mrs. Rhee had prized, unfurl the *yo,* and sleep, and in sleep, return to a past that never quite ended for anyone. She contemplated Mrs. Rhee's photograph, her salty smile, the brown smudge of a mole on the woman's chin.

Within a half hour, she rifled through the closet's woolly sweaters, telling herself that she must help this hopeless man coordinate, though she knew what she wanted. She pushed to the back of the closet and found what had been left behind: churchy floral dresses, ruffled blouses. And though it was inappropriate—no, invasive—she tried on one of the polyester washing-machine-safe dresses. She pinned her hair to the right and smoothed it into place until the mirror gratified her. Finally, she was freed from herself.

The new Mrs. Shin set the robot at a low level, and thrust the paddle at the table. The balls came at her like a relentless argument. She missed, missed, struck. The dress soon cleaved to her like plastic kitchen wrap. After a time the machine spawned only gurgling sounds. Sweat bubbled on her upper lip and hair fused to her cheekbones. Tired but refreshed, she tossed the paddle across the table. It collided with the net.

She traced the table's crude divisions, one of the good, simple things left from a life that had gone wrong. She, too, understood escape.

"Sleeping under the table," she said. "It's beautiful."

Her hand was feeling across her back for the zipper when the bedroom door clicked open. He had returned earlier than he had said he would.

"You didn't go to practice," she said.

"How, how devious," he stuttered. "How dare you insult me?"

"I had no right to . . ." With her head bowed, she fell to her knees, one at a time.

He said, "Please, Mrs. Shin. This isn't the theater . . ." He walked past, then swiveled back, his fingers twitching. "You wanted to play, let's play."

She remained on her knees. "You should slap me," she said. She offered him her body.

"I would never hurt a woman."

He wanted to hit her, she could tell; his hands were balled into bony fists.

"You're angry." Her entire body was prepared. She leaned toward him. "You'll feel better, after."

Instead he punched the wall, wincing even as he did it.

"Mr. Rhee!"

He wiggled the hand in the air, still shaking. "Don't ever, ever speak like that again, please."

"You were so angry." She stood, slowly. "I only asked for what I deserved."

After they iced and wrapped the modest spectacle of his swelling hand, and he washed off what must have been the day's humiliations, he opened a bottle of rice wine. They sank into the sofa by a stack of jigsaw puzzles and a checkered *baduk* board—hobbies of a solitary person.

The thimble-size *soju* glass clattered as Mr. Rhee set it down.

The paper lampshade above them swung, then rocked to a stop. She did not remove his hand when he laid it on hers.

After Mr. Rhee's visit, the detective made regular reports to Mrs. Shin. He told her of his own difficulties immigrating eight years ago when he had abruptly decided to leave accountancy and leave Seoul. "I opened a store and before the first year was over, I had a bullet in me." His left hand became a gun that jabbed at his right shoulder. "And my—boy, he almost dropped out in his first semester at university." He looked excited, almost wistful, as he recalled those years of hardship, and she thought it must be possible for the past to someday be rendered harmless. It ended happily, he assured her, as it will for you. The detective's overtures of friendliness surprised her almost as much as the Ping-Pong lessons Mr. Rhee insisted on, and she could only wonder at how unknowable man was. As for her Ping-Pong game, it improved rapidly. Mr. Rhee trained her to use a pimple-surfaced rubber paddle, then a sponge-covered one for topspin, and even monitored her practice hours. They went on a picnic where they were surrounded by geese the size of her daughter; they held hands and rode a creaking roller coaster on the Santa Monica promenade, facing the setting sun while holding hands and laughing, as if they were a young couple with a long, hopeful future ahead of them. Sometimes she woke up under the Ping-Pong table with her hair in the thicket of his pubic hair, though she insisted they still shower separately, like civilized people. Her own attempt at updating Mr. Rhee's wardrobe was a quiet failure.

Each pleasant, uneventful night passed much like the next. It was as if another her was married again with an actual future ahead, as if there was the possibility of love. Except that none of it felt real until she stepped outside of the house for a walk and saw the tidy suburban landscape sprawled out in front of her, and heard a nation of people of all colors speaking a language that wasn't hers.

In November, Detective Pak called.

"I've located your daughter," he said.

She couldn't speak. She had to remind herself to breathe, one, two, as she imagined her daughter's sleeping face. The memory was frozen, a photograph that had replaced her actual daughter's face as unpredictable as the flight pattern of a moth; and though she willed the image to move and become alive for her again, the image dominated and the sleeping face remained slightly puzzled, with eyebrows raised as if the face had never experienced another expression. That was the last time Mrs. Shin had seen her daughter.

After a swallow of coffee, in the same unhurried voice, Detective Pak told her Yuri's home address in Beverly Hills, three blocks from the school she attended.

She traced the scribbled address with her index finger, not quite believing it to be real. More than four years had passed since she had touched her daughter, four years that had taken away her child, and her husband, from her. Those four years—they were not real to her, either. She began wondering what to wear—the navy skirt suit or the forest green wraparound dress?—already anxious. She had faith in appearances.

"Thank you," she said. "Thank you, thank you."

"Well," he said, "you're only getting what you deserve."

She drew back from the phone. "You're quite right, yes."

Softer this time, he said, "I also lost my children . . . It was a terrible choice to have to make, a necessary loss."

Startled, she waited for him to continue. But he wished her the best, then there was the click of the receiver.

Children dressed in clothes as colorful as marbles spilled out across the yard. Through the aluminum fence built so high she could not touch its top, she watched her daughter's life: the queue of American children waiting to play (Queuing! Children!), the jungle gym made for larger bodies, these harsh, glottal syllables, the few Asian faces, boys and girls, that belonged to bodies moving with an ease that she had thought belonged only to men.

She had dressed up for her daughter as if for an interview. But despite her navy pin-striped suit and her supple leather shoes and purse, the horizontal lines of the fence now imprinted on her face made her look unhinged. Its hot metal pricked her skin. The crowds thinned as parents picked up their children. She continued looking.

Then there was Yuri. Mrs. Shin held herself; she began rocking back and forth, the pressure of feeling in her heart, her feet, her stomach, so strong her body would explode if she did not contain it. Yuri was clustered with other second grade girls, two formidable fists on the hips of designer jeans that Mrs. Shin recognized by the detailing on the pockets. Her face was still round, pumpkin-shaped like Mrs. Shin's, and her darkly alert eyes were her father's, but her hair had lightened to a nutty brown. She was so adult, not the same girl who had promenaded each of her toys for guests. When her friends began a round of hopscotch, Yuri sighed as she joined in, as if surrendering to their nonsense.

Her daughter's deportment was a reprimand. Yuri had not stopped for time. The girl that Mrs. Shin had expected was changed, anchored by confidence, by friends, by a gaze that took in the playground as if she owned it—her father's gaze. Somehow she had stopped being the girl who looked for her mother everywhere, and somehow, while some other woman had taken care of her, she had grown. Mrs. Shin's explanations—the years it took to cobble a life together and hoard the money to return to Yuri—all of it became excuses that might no longer be relevant.

Still, she called out her daughter's name; Yuri only continued to look periodically from the hopscotch to the parking lot. Only when Mrs. Shin tossed a pebble her way did her daughter look up and look around. She saw her mother.

Yuri had been three when her parents separated; she shyly regarded her mother as if she were a distant relation.

"Yuri," she said.

"My American name is Grace," said Yuri. She rocked on her heels, excited and afraid, then Mrs. Shin saw that she was still a child.

"You were Yuri first," she said, her voice weighted, despite herself, with reproach.

"I know who I am," Yuri said. "I'm called Grace most of the time."

Her face was ugly with a stubbornness Mrs. Shin knew as her own, and she felt great pity and love for her daughter; the years ahead would work to undo her girlish certainty.

"Come to your mother," Mrs. Shin said. "I won't hurt you."

"Hurt me?" Yuri looked as if she had not considered this a possibility.

Mrs. Shin had enough of talking. She saw her daughter moving farther and farther from her, so far that soon enough she would be untouchable, moored to this foreign land of perennial drought and swimming pools.

She jogged to the corner of the fence, then turned, her arms out to her daughter, but Yuri ran, ran away—toward the parking lot. Mrs. Shin followed, first trotting in her heels, then running. What lies had they told her daughter?

Yuri rapped on a black sedan's tinted window with her fists. The door clicked open and Yuri's terrified face disappeared behind it, but Mrs. Shin caught the door. One acrylic nail ripped off, her wrist bent backward, but the door swung open, and forestalled her exile.

In the rearview mirror, her ex-husband's gaze stabbed into her. She sank into the leather seat and crossed her legs, ready to negotiate.

His nose flared. "What are you doing? Where did you find her?"

"It's not my fault," Yuri said. She recoiled from her mother, demonstrating where her loyalties lay.

Mrs. Shin's eyes shifted from him to her daughter, her world suddenly unclear. It was too much for her—her husband, her daughter, the car a reliquary of their failings. She reached into her purse, snapped a bamboo fan open, and cooled herself.

"Still living on your family's money, are you?" she said. "You never could take care of yourself."

"Why don't you wait outside, mushroom," Yuri's father said. "Go play with your friends. We'll pick up Mother from the doctor's soon enough."

Yuri opened the door and retreated. She sat primly within a

few feet of the car. She leaned over as if practicing for an earthquake drill, her eyes riveted to the spokes of the tires. She seemed
too afraid to blink.

"*Sheebal.*" He cursed, spraying spit onto the mirror. "Yuri
finally gets used to her new mother and here you come with your
desires and disturb everything."

"After four years a mother finds her kidnapped daughter." Her
hands gripped the handle of the door as she watched her daughter
outside. "How disturbed is that?"

"Still acting up, acting out." But there was a lubricant heat to
his voice, as if some latch had loosened. "Kidnapped? All we did
was move."

Mrs. Shin's eyes dragged from Yuri back to the mirror.

"Do you beat her?"

"You know I wouldn't touch Yuri."

She twisted the silk fan until the wooden frame snapped in
two. She shuddered at herself in the mirror, a woman with eyes
aflame. She had come to see her daughter; she had. She had not
left Korea to be this other woman again.

"I mean, do you beat *her*?"

He studied Mrs. Shin. "That's not for you to know."

"You must help me." She couldn't stop herself. "You made me
the way I am."

"No one made you but God."

"When we first met, you said—"

"We were an earthquake for each other."

She touched his shoulder. Her palm tingled; he jerked away.

"I was thirty and you gave me—what? Fire, and nothing will
ever wake me up again."

He slumped against the steering wheel. She waited.

"What do you want from me, woman?"

"Hit me. No one can see us."

"Find yourself a gentle lamb." His voice had brittled up, was careful again. "Someone quiet you can share your old age with."

"I've tried." Her nails scraped into her scalp. "Oh, I'm trying."

"You'll get used to it."

"Like I got used to you."

His large right hand made a perfect fist before he composed himself.

He finally faced her.

"If you don't leave now, Yuri will finally learn what kind of mother she has." His voice was in control, as smooth as a luxury car engine. "She's only a child—what will that knowledge do to her?"

The clock had mercifully stopped its ticking. Dust motes spun, zigzagged across the cloth-covered sewing machine, the love seat, the militant rows of perfume bottles on the armoire, settled, then lifted. Mrs. Shin stayed hidden under the tweed comforter as she had for the past few hours or days. It was night, it was day; it was America, it was Korea; it was nowhere, and she was no one. She would not be able to manage Mr. Rhee's sympathetic gaze.

When she roused herself, she stared out at dusty beams of white light, wondering what they were, until she realized, of course, they were coming from streetlights. Sweet rice and spicy cabbage stew smells saturated the room. Mr. Rhee must be making dinner; he must be tidying up the kitchen, thinking of clearing off a bookshelf for her, maybe hoping for a genteel poke before bed. She pulled her useless clothes off their hangers and carpeted the floor with silk and cashmere. In the mirror, she stared spitefully at her hand-stitched jacket, the garnet brooch adorning her chest. She stripped, cupped her forty-six-year-old breasts. These lumps had nourished a baby but were still ugly, sick breasts, an aging body still betraying her with its monstrous desires. It was better that Yuri had not wanted her.

She removed scissors from her sewing basket and held it to a swatch of her hair. She cut deliberately, evenly, then flung hair at her image. "I hate you," she said. "I hate you," she said louder, then even louder until she was screaming.

By the time Mr. Rhee pounded on the door, she had stabbed the cushions of the love seat, swept the perfume bottles to the floor. She took her sewing scissors and ran the edge along the back of her thigh. The pain erased all grief, stripped her of camouflage. A wound so bright it looked pasted on blossomed on her leg. There was no symmetry yet, so she ran the scissors down the other thigh.

"Mrs. Shin!" A distant voice tried to reach her, but she was beyond reaching. There was only the world narrowing to predictable pinpoints of pain. She took off her thin belt and tried it against her back. She was becoming herself again, loving herself, as the door crashed down like a bomb and Mr. Rhee crawled through, his hands blindly pushed out in front of him. But even as he reached for Mrs. Shin, my darling, my love, her wounded body continued its ancient song.

AT THE EDGE OF THE WORLD

H<small>IS NAME WAS</small> Myeongseok Lee at home and Mark Lee at school, he was nine years old, and he knew everything. He knew that in Peru one bush housed more ant species than all of the United Kingdom, and that rain forests above three thousand feet were called cloud forests. That dogs had nose prints the way humans had fingerprints, that a violin contained more than seventy pieces of wood, and that ninety-nine percent of what people bought they didn't use after six months. He knew that his sixth grade teacher, Mrs. Whitney, tried to make him skip another grade because he corrected her grammar mistakes out loud and napped during sharing time, and that his parents were melancholy when they ordered him pizza for dinner instead of making rice, or spoke quietly about their hometown and family that might be dead or alive, they would never know, or about America passing the North Korean Human Rights Act in 2004, but so far had let only two hundred of their people—only two hundred, including their family!—into the country. He knew that Roberto the bully was right—that Mark's father couldn't *really* love him because he wasn't his real father. He knew you were supposed to have friends but he didn't care. He knew that President Lincoln was so depressed he was afraid of carrying a penknife in case he might kill himself, and that William Taft was the world's heaviest president ever. Today was May 17, 2009. He knew everything.

For example, no matter how normal his parents pretended they were, he knew they were different. Sure they worked at normal jobs, his mother as a waitress in a *galbi* restaurant and his stepfather exterminating bugs and managing the duplex they lived in. His mother read him Korean folktales and his father taught him algebra, his oversize dandelion head wagging on the short stalk of his body, and though Mark spotted shortcuts that would save a calculation or two, he feigned confusion so his father could feel helpful. Then suddenly the State Department would call, or his father would notice someone following their used Kia. Last week an official in charge of the four, now three, North Koreans in Los Angeles County—he, his mother, his father, and a man who had killed himself last year—visited. He congratulated them on how quickly they had adapted, calling them "model refugee cases." His father's eyebrows knotted together, but he smiled and said, "I've never considered myself some case," then changed the subject. Once, his father had believed in the North Korean leader Kim Jong-il the way the Korean immigrant community around them believed in God.

"Is he better than his dad, Kim Il-sung?" Mark asked that night at the dinner table.

"He's a very, very bad man," his father said as quietly as his shuffle, his signature on paper, *Choecheol Ra,* and the neutral col-

ors he wore that made him resemble an animal seeking camouflage.

"How bad?" Mark said now, and leaned into the marinated
beef insulting his vegetarian eyes. "Any bloody thumbs?"

His father's Adam's apple danced. He said, "There was a
school lesson they taught us that went, 'One plus one equals two
dead Americans.'"

His mother made a nervous, tickling motion with her hand on
her throat. Nothing scared her but the past. She said, "Myeongseok's only nine. Don't pollute him."

His father said, "Then who's ever going to know?"

She said decisively, "Your problem is you live in the past."

His father planted a kiss on the back of her palm. She blushed.

"I'm happy! If that's what you want," his father said. "Of course
I'm happy all the time."

On May 22, the most important day of the year, since it was the
day Mark was born, new renters to their duplex knocked on their
door. A woman bowed, pausing as she dipped down ballerina-
style, then rose. Her dress reminded him of a cloud. Though
everything looked wrong about her—the sharp nose against the
pillowy softness of her face, her snowy head of hair and wispy
eyebrows—she carried herself with a grace more swan than
woman. Hiding behind her were puzzle fragments of a girl his
age. Mark looked for a limp, a missing finger, a wig. That was
their neighborhood—everyone was missing something.

"Come in!" his mother boomed, her voice fiercely friendly,
squeezing her bountiful, three-tiered waterfall of a stomach, as

she greeted them. When she wasn't wearing makeup or a dress, people thought she was a man.

The woman dropped the basket of rice cakes in her hand, but his father caught it, then winked at Mark.

"I'm pleased to meet you for the first time," the woman said, her lips barely moving as she spoke. "We've come for the keys."

"Oh, don't run away, have some cake," his mother said, and tugged the woman into the house by the arm. "Wouldn't your granddaughter like some cake? It's our son's birthday."

The woman said in that feathery voice, "This is my daughter."

His mother looked displeased at being contradicted. She expected obedience. His father tugged nervously at his belt; Mark spotted a twenty-dollar bill protruding out of his father's sock. His father kept money in the strangest places.

His father said, "Please save us. You'll be doing our health a favor if you help us with my son's cake meant for twelve people."

Behind the clownish twist of his father's face, there was a carefulness as he studied them, as he studied all strangers, like a textbook.

The woman regarded his father with suspicion. Mark was used to this. His father looked far too young to be his father. His mother was the same. She had been sixteen in China when a farmer she had been sold to made her a baby, which was Mark. Once, she had said, "Thank the Lord, the man hasn't left a trace in my son." But age was age, and cake was cake. His new purple cape flared behind him as he ran backward, so these strangers wouldn't take more than their proper share of the cake that he'd especially requested with the frosted letters SAY NO TO PLASTIC.

The girl stepped out from behind her mother's back, a finger in her mouth, her eyes on his cake. Mark stopped breathing. She looked like a cartoon character: copper pennies for eyes, two pigtails as aerodynamic as rockets, a fancy dress resembling lemon meringue that covered nine-tenths of her, making the friendly sun her nemesis. He stared at her, a girl so serious she seemed afraid to smile, while his mother brought out plates and a stinky tea that was supposedly good for your health. The girl stared back.

They found a place to sit despite his mother's habit of hoarding chairs, sofas, and old magazines that neighbors threw out. Once, she had become enraged after finding half a rotting peach in the refrigerator. "Even animals don't waste!" she'd said.

The old people began talking in careful, fake-friendly voices. "Your daughter's so tall . . ." "Arrived from Korea a week ago . . ." "This is a good country," his mother said, though after they had arrived from the Bangkok detention center four years ago she never left the Los Angeles Koreatown so never *really* needed to speak English, especially with Mark as translator, interpreter, and the youngest personal secretary in history. His mother fired away with questions. She liked to know what was what. Husband, hometown, hobbies, work.

"I'm a shaman, widowed," the woman said, each syllable separated, her head tipping higher with each word. "You should know this about us."

"Jesus saved us," his mother said emphatically. "I don't do shamanism."

His father, embarrassed, poured more stinky tea. He said, "Everyone's welcome here."

The woman sat, hands folded impassively together, her eyes watching and waiting.

Mark asked, "What does a shaman do?" He only remembered muddy photographs of ceremonial food at an altar and an old woman moving a paper boat over a white strip of cloth.

His mother said, "Keep quiet!"

His father said, "He's just curious."

The girl had gone very still, like her mother; she was watching the old people.

"What's your name?" Mark asked her, then saw that, like her mother, she didn't understand English, so he switched to Korean.

"I'm Chanhee," she said. The words came out crisp but slow, as if she weren't used to talking.

"And, little boy"—the girl's mother turned to him with her cheerless smile—"what's that around your neck?"

"I'm not little." Mark pushed up the glasses he had begged his mother to buy so he would look more intellectual. "I'm average height for my age, which today is now ten, so I'm much too old to be a boy. This is a stethoscope."

"He's going to be a doctor," his mother said.

"I'm going to be a heart surgeon and buy Omma and Appa a house in Beverly Hills."

"It's good to have a son!" his father said, and cut him the best slice of cake crowned by two plastic bags made of sooty icing.

They began talking more quietly, their bodies turned away from Mark.

"You're weird," Chanhee said, faster this time.

He studied his feet. "Depends on your definition of *weird*."

He knew small talk was important to fueling a conversation, so he said, "You know the twenty-ninth U.S. president, Woodrow

Wilson? He used to carry a stomach pump with him everywhere he went, his digestion was that bad."

She shot back with, "Can you wiggle your ears?"

She made her white lobes flutter like pale butterflies.

Her mother, his mother, his father, all of them were lost to the importance of the moment when Chanhee's ears went pink as they tilted his way. She said shyly, "If I'm your friend, will you check me with your steth— That thing around your neck?"

A friend. So what if there were oil wars in Iraq, ritual dolphin murders in Denmark, Los Angeles pollution blackening his lungs? He had Chanhee as a friend. But that night his mother said that a shaman sounded like trouble.

"It's blasphemous," she said. "It'll bring us bad fortune to live near someone talking to the dead."

She threatened to kick the new renters out. His father, uncharacteristically, refused. His father was an atheist, even if it was the church that had helped them with free counseling, jars of kimchi and shopping bags crammed with clothes, and finding jobs. "Kim Jong-il was enough worship for me," his father would mutter when his mother wasn't around.

"You women should understand," he said. "She's new to America. Remember she'll have to fight for herself and her daughter, and don't you know what that's like, fighting for your family's life?"

"I know, I know, don't I know!" his mother said, her words punching the air. "What should we have for dinner?"

"All she's doing is trying to help people," his father said.

"Just who can a shaman help?" his mother said. "I see what happens when they charge the price of a cow and pretend to talk to the dead. People practically give their money away when it doesn't change anything."

To Mark's relief, his father got in the last word.

The next time Mark saw Chanhee, she waved, then rushed into her side of the house. Their white door identical to Mark's swung open and closed, back and forth, as if it couldn't decide what it wanted to be. He smelled incense and heard the ping of drumming that his mother would complain about all summer.

He paced, his legs outstretched like a goose-stepping soldier. He crushed weeds, twisted the neck of a prickly poppy with his hands. He was smart and had a smile as winning as chocolate-covered marshmallows. He didn't understand why kids tried to pull off his pants or walked behind him, poking between the crack of his buttocks with a stick. Once, they'd lifted the sewer lid and left him down in the mucky dark for half an hour, trying to scare him, but he didn't scare. Not much. He had loudly recited the names of all the counties in Southern California until the boys said, "Someone'll hear him!" and pulled him out. He didn't know why Chanhee would change her mind about him.

He went back to his house and faked being his regular brilliant self.

At night he couldn't sleep. He considered stabbing himself with his father's nose-hair scissors, drinking laundry detergent mixed with Kool-Aid. His goodbye note would have to be read at his funeral. He scouted the house. In the kitchen he saw his father at the table without the lights on. His face was veiled with shadows, and in front of him was a tidy pyramid of unopened beer cans. He must have been carrying heavy equipment all day; he rubbed at his shoulder hard enough to leave a bruise. There was something ruined about his posture, like the brick remains of a demolished building. His father didn't notice Mark—he wanted very much to be noticed. Maybe he should give his father a hug and cheer him up the way his mother seemed so simply, so foolishly, to respond to Mark, but his father and he had never been that way with each other; there had always been this politeness that made Mark feel as if his father were training to be a father and he were training to be his son. He was afraid of the way his father's face shrank into a despairing mask, as if this were his true face, and not the quiet man who was always laughing at his mother's plans and at the universe. He started tiptoeing back to his room.

His father looked up at Mark's first step. His father smiled—or tried to smile. "This is what happens when Omma doesn't send the boys to bed."

"Appa, what were you doing outside?"

His father cracked open a can. "I miss my family."

He meant the family he had had in North Korea that seemed more important to him than Mark, and they weren't even here.

"Tell the story about how I almost died," Mark said.

It was his favorite story, the one about how his mother and he had escaped the truck returning them to the North Korean border, where death awaited him; the North Korean authorities prized pure Korean bloodlines and despised babies born from Chinese men. But after a car crash and a sympathetic local's help, they had escaped. His parents had later met in China, walked across the entire country, finally carrying Mark through the jungles of Laos with no maps, no compass, just a route in their heads they had memorized. It was a good story because it was a happy story.

His father gestured to the chair beside him, which relieved Mark enormously. Except his father said, "It's wrong how we pretend we keep going forward."

"But we *are* going forward," Mark said. "Tomorrow isn't today and today isn't yesterday."

The silence in the room spread and became part of the vast black penumbra outside the window, where danger lived; he wanted to find shelter in his father's arms, but the darkness of his father's face was no friendlier than the darkness outside.

Finally his father said, "People think an exterminator is a terrible job. At church they keep trying to find me better work, but this is really all right with me. You know why, Myeongseok?"

Mark couldn't think of a single valid reason for choosing face-to-face contact with a cockroach, an insect that could stay alive for over two weeks *after* it had been beheaded. A fact he wished he didn't know.

"It doesn't pretend to be anything it isn't. You fight the termites, the rats, the ants, you pretend that with your uniform and goggles and respirator and chemicals you're in control, though you know the entire time you're going nowhere. It's what we do every day, pretend we're going somewhere."

His voice dipped so Mark could no longer hear his father muttering.

Late each night Mark began getting up for a glass of milk. But each time he stole to the kitchen, hoping not to see his father, there he would be in the dark, his ear turned upward, listening to the silence.

———

In June summer vacation began. His parents were at work and Mark was supposed to be at a math day camp funded by the Korean Presbyterian church his mother diligently attended. But after a boy aimed a softball to strike Mark in the eye, he worked out a deal with his parents and attended the academic morning classes and skipped the dreary afternoon activities like pottery and softball for dummies; he had told his mother a love-struck girl was stalking him, and for his safety, he had better stay off the field.

She wrapped his entire head up the way he asked so he looked as sinister as an Egyptian mummy.

Who is this girl?" she demanded. Her face was a black cumulonimbus cloud. "Do I know her mother?"

He patted her leg. "I'm okeydokey," he said in English, which always got her off his back. "It doesn't hurt *that* much."

"Now it looks like you survived brain surgery," she said.

He liked that even better than being a mummy, so he allowed her to kiss his bandaged forehead.

He watched for Chanhee. Their gauzy white curtains fluttered like ghosts. The neighborhood was so nature-unfriendly that there wasn't a bird in sight, not even a pigeon. The grass was the color of cement. His mother was grateful, praising God for this neighborhood that was the grit of liquor stores and gang members signing the walls, lottery machines where people lined up as if for a concert, and a battalion of languages—*battalion,* one of his new favorite words—competing with one another. Even the telephone box was graffitied with THESE ARE THE UNDYING VOICES OF THE PEOPLE. YOUS THE BASTARDS OF THE WORLD. *CHICA, ESTOY ENTIENDO.* PROPAGANDA

OF THE UNHEARD. Sometimes he wondered if the same lonely person was writing back and forth to himself. He watched cars growl past. The heartbreaking melody of the elusive ice-cream truck and the blur of pickup trucks loaded with swap meet goods, grandfathers squatting on the stoops of houses who told him they were waiting to die. He watched people trickle in and out of Chanhee's house. Then as June became July, more people visited the neighbors' home.

"For people new to America," his mother said, "they have a lot of friends."

His father picked up the paper and covered his face. "She's a nice person," he said.

"How do you know?"

The sound of cymbals clanging next door crashed into their conversation.

"We're neighbors. A friendly talk here and there—what's wrong with that?"

"It's not right, what they do. It's not good for you to associate with them." Her voice rose as she spoke, becoming shrill. "It's bad memories, and there's enough worries without them."

She persisted until his father threw the paper down.

As usual Mark had to mediate their argument. Even though he knew the answer, he asked, "What's a prostitute?" Which got them to behave themselves.

The sun beat down. Chanhee wore a lot of red. Red T-shirts so old that the ironed-on letters were peeling off: ETTY OOP, MAR MONRO, always with red patent leather shoes. In his waiting he was getting a tan though he'd never even been to the Pacific Ocean, which was rumored to be very close, somewhere to the west. He was about to give up on Chanhee when she materialized and took away the Webster's dictionary he was reading—he'd gotten up to *M* so far—and balanced it on her fingertips.

She said, "It's true. You don't have any friends."

He scrutinized a spot of dirt under his fingernail and wished he had taken the dreaded bath the night before.

"Well," she added, "I don't, either."

He lingered every day for her. When she emerged from her house, it was the best day since the Republicans left office; and when she was convinced that bacteria were devouring her intestines or that the sun would give her eye cancer, and she mournfully drew the curtains, it was the worst day since his favorite movie theater with three-dollar seats on Wednesdays raised prices on caramel popcorn, which his mother now refused to buy him. But Chanhee could touch her nose with her tongue, played a mean game of Starcraft, and best, she listened to him recite his favorite words from the dictionary and asked him how to use *nascent* and *numinous* in a sentence.

The first time they kissed, Chanhee and Mark were in his room, Spartan clean the way he liked it. Library books (so he didn't kill more trees) on one long shelf were organized by shape, color, subject. He allowed himself a few possessions. One puppet, one cape, one abacus, a life-size poster of all the U.S. presidents squeezed together, with the younger George Bush's face whited out to make room for Mark's head shot; one knapsack in case he ever had somewhere to go.

"Why American presidents?" she asked. "You're not American."

He said, "We *live* here."

She said gravely, "But will they let us stay?"

"Someday," he promised, "when I have a lot of hair on my chin, I'll make lots of money, be made president, and I'll marry you, and no one will ever make us leave."

She said, "What if you never grow hair?," ungrateful for his generous gesture.

"My father shaves twice a day," he said. Which wasn't entirely true.

"You promise?" She puckered her lips and said fiercely, "Remember, you promised."

She was waiting for him to kiss her. The only girl he had ever kissed was his mother, and his mother was not a girl. He picked up his Burmese puppet and hugged it.

She said, "Turn your face to me," so he did.

"Close your eyes, silly," she said, so he did.

A moment later, he felt her hair feathery against his lips full with the taste of blackberries, then he felt her lips. There was a summery dryness to them, as unsentimental and careful as she was.

"Okeydokey!" he said, and wiped away the kiss.

The day of their second kiss, it was August, the streets shimmered with heat, and being outside was a punishment. Chanhee's house had a cool underground feeling, less like Los Angeles and more a long-lost world from the other side of the ocean. Her mother had brought that world with her in carved masks, silk scrolls of horned demons and men with titanic bellies, and celadon vases with tiny painted cranes, which made Mark want to get his markers and fill the vast white spaces that the artist had neglected. The incense snaking through the hall was familiar, as was the smell of Chanhee's shampoo and the tinning of drums and wailing songs he'd gotten used to, now even enjoyed.

Once in her room, all frills and bright cushions, she said, "Well, future husband, we have to practice."

So they did. He was dizzy. She said they had done a better job than the first time. She brought icy cans of Coke from the kitchen, and though the evil company had used slave labor in Nazi Germany and murdered trade union leaders, Mark pretended it was delicious.

They became energetic.

"Can you do this?"

After jumping to his favorite K-pop CD that he'd brought, she slid into the splits.

For Chanhee, he pushed his legs apart as far as they would go. Which was not very far. Chanhee was pulling one of his legs, and he was holding on to her bedpost and groaning, when he heard his father's voice.

Chanhee rushed to the door and blocked it with her arms and legs in an X shape. She said, "We shouldn't."

"Why's my *appa* here?"

She looked nervous, guilty.

"I'm staying here," she said, "the way I'm supposed to when Omma's working."

Mark tickled her until she balled up on the floor, then left. What was his father doing? He wanted to know and he didn't want to know.

He pushed the door open.

There was the shaman pacing, her pale face shimmering with sweat. "We invite you to come and enter me," she said, her face raised to the ceiling. "Your little brother, Choecheol Ra, misses you." His father was listening so intently, he didn't notice Mark. She jumped violently as if possessed, and her ramie *hanbok* and headdress trembled. The few people present were shadows. An altar was loaded with candles, and swords gleamed with their blades rising from a large vase, like flowers. There were plates of sliced pork, Asian pears, rice cakes, uncooked grain, a pig's head on a platter, its eyes slit as if about to open. The pig looked alive. It scared Mark, and he wanted to touch it. In the middle of all this, there was his father, on his knees like a child being punished, and the shaman spitting chants onto his back. Mark touched his father's thigh; he was pushed away. The shaman turned her ear up as if she were listening to the heavens.

"I'm here, little brother," she said in a young boy's voice. "Don't worry about me, I'm all right." She slapped a folding fan against her palm.

Mark slid to the floor. He said, "What are you doing to my *appa*?"

She spun around his father, shaking her fan to the hourglass drum that a man sitting on the floor beat, left side then right, with a rod. A woman in a white *hanbok* clanged at a handheld gong. His father leaned forward as the shaman uttered scraps of old-fashioned words between a song and an incantation. "None of it was your fault," she said, striking her father's back with a fan. Mark felt seasick and afraid as she leaped across the room, and voice after voice seemed to enter his father and send him capsizing to the floor.

It was getting dark. His father cried as he talked to his dead older brother, holding on to a branch with leaves in his hand and shaking it into a bowl of uncooked rice grains. There was more chanting as Mark sat at the door hugging his knees, worried that his mother would come back early from English class and never forgive his father, and they would not be a family anymore.

When the shaman tried to take the branch—some kind of spirit wand—from his father, he wouldn't let go. Instead he said, *"Sarang haeyo,"* his lips making a confession of love toward the ceiling. He was remote and lonely, again the late-night stranger in the kitchen. His father curled up on the floor, his knees to his chest, clutching at the wand with both hands. Mark wondered and feared at the world that filled his father with such trembling.

"Sarang haeyo," his father said again to an invisible person. I love you.

His father had once untied Mark from a telephone pole on his way home and didn't press him when Mark said, "You must *never* talk about today," but the next time he got off the school bus, a Korean granny neighbor of theirs was waiting to escort him home. When he begged, his father had sponsored two sheep for him in Morocco and told his mother he had purchased one, and sometimes Mark woke up and saw his father watching over him, his hand feathering through his hair. Still, not once had his father ever said those words to him.

Mark's father could never keep a secret from his mother. The ninth commandment said, Thou shalt not lie. The Arabic saying was that lying and stealing are next-door neighbors to each other. Mark also favored honesty, but within reason. When his father decided to confess just where he had been that Monday afternoon when he should have been at work, the results were predictably disastrous. His mother withdrew his father's rice bowl before he had begun eating breakfast. She cleared his utensils and pushed the dishes of pickled vegetables and mountain roots away from his side of the table.

"You've chewed away a small fortune on a superstition. I know how much a *kut* costs!"

His father's chin dropped down to his neck. "My brother was there—"

"I work and clean and cook so you can give away money to talk to the dead. Your brother's not here—he's dead! He's nowhere!"

Mark was shocked; he had assumed these were chores that she had enjoyed. His father put his head down on the table; in the August heat, his mother shivered.

"This is our country now." She jabbed at the tiled floor below her. "But it isn't enough for you to live in the shadows. You have to bring my Myeongseok there with you."

"I felt him, my brother!" his father said. "For just a little while, I felt him there. I won't pretend our lives didn't happen—"

His mother blasted through his words.

"You think too much," she said, louder now. "He's dead. They're all dead. Just don't think!"

She was crying. It was the first time Mark had ever seen her cry. She said she was not going to let her son be infected by his inability to live in the present. There was more.

"Appa," Mark finally said, "you said that Omma was your translator for the world.

"And, Omma, you said Appa was the gentlest man you know. You said Appa knew what mattered."

In this way, he tried to remind them of their obligations.

"Don't protect him," his mother said. "He's not even your biological father."

His father's hands went up, as if he'd been hit.

"He's my son, too. That's what we agreed," he said. "We made this family together . . ."

But Mark didn't have a real father. He had emerged from his mother's life in China as mysteriously as the idea of immaculate conception. There was only this man who could study a single tweedy sparrow for hours and make a protruding monkey jaw face that made the real monkey look fake. A man who spoke in sharp Mandarin sentences learned from years living in hiding in China, a man who told stories about his life as if they had happened to someone else. This was his father.

For a time his parents only spoke to each other through Mark. He didn't like these people anymore as his father became more depressed, and his mother became angrier. They conspired to make his life miserable by filling the house with his father's growing gloom and his mother's continual diatribes; they were being so unreasonable. As if they didn't have a growing child on their hands. As if he didn't matter to them anymore.

He was feeling rebellious. At dinner he tapped his glass and announced his engagement to Chanhee Roh.

"That's illegal at your age," his mother said. "You won't remember the girl's name by sixteen."

He told her that was impossible. She said he should make some forward-looking friends.

"From now on," she said, "you're not allowed to see Chanhee at all."

She lit up with relief at the prospect of Chanhee's banishment. When Mark looked at his father for help, his father spooned vegetable curry into his mouth and chewed, his mouth moving in a circle like a cow. He felt betrayed. He couldn't eat; he was heroic with worry. Romeo and Juliet. Chunyang and Mongryeong. He wasn't the first to experience families conspiring to keep love apart. The next day he malingered in bed. He refused food.

His mother sighed. "We didn't have food, and he's choosing to starve for a girl whose name he won't remember in two months."

His father said, "Don't forget you're angry at me, not Myeong-seok."

Mark crossed his arms across his chest. "I'm a person of principles."

She slapped him, her hand as light as a young palm leaf on his cheek so it wasn't much of a slap, and told him to apologize.

He straightened up in bed. "Did you know that even George Washington—"

"I don't know anyone like that," his mother said.

"—that even America's first president was scared of his mother?"

On Sunday his mother locked him in the car after he threatened to tell the pastor that she stole rolls of toilet paper from the church bathroom. He no longer made an effort to entertain and educate his parents. Sometimes he missed the toilet when peeing, there was still nothing for him to shave, and he had only a yellow belt in tae kwon do after two years of lessons, but someday, oh, some glorious day, he vowed, he would protect the one he loved.

The calendar informed him that it had been one week since the world became different. It felt like a year. Around then his mother reserved a motel room near the Grand Canyon's North Rim for a family trip. The Grand Canyon. One of those places his mother was always talking about. She practically sang those words as if it were going to save their lives. When Mark said he wouldn't go without Chanhee, she lifted him one-handed out of his chair and deposited him in the backseat of the car. "You're going," she said. "And you're going to enjoy yourself."

In the middle of a concrete motel room pretending to be a log cabin, Mark unpacked a blanket and folding chair to build a tent for himself. His mother unloaded the entire kitchen from the car, including a portable gas burner, sneaking in two grocery bags at a time so the motel manager wouldn't catch her. As they rattled about unpacking, his mother and father pretended that they were no longer angry at each other. Chanhee wasn't there, and the five days ahead looked long.

He lay in the tent and folded his hands across his chest like a vampire. The North Rim was higher than the South Rim by eleven hundred feet, the Colorado River moved at four miles an hour, but there was no one to share all this with. He missed his quilt and firm mattress, he missed people to talk to. He didn't like camping after all, so he crawled out of the tent. The clock said he had been cloistered for exactly eighteen minutes.

"I'm not going anywhere special," his father said.

"So why can't I go with you?" His mother looked upset. "Let cats be cats and dogs be dogs—I'm not the one dragging us back to where we began."

"Stop it. Now."

She nodded, her head slowly descending, ascending.

I'm so afraid," she said. "I don't know why."

"Tomorrow," he said firmly. "We'll go hiking. We'll have a good time tomorrow, our family."

He put on his brown jacket, brown socks, brown shoes. Hunched over, his father looked smaller than he was, and it was strange to think that in a year or two, Mark would be taller than his father.

"This is a time to be alone," he said. "You know what day it is for me today."

She didn't push further. He opened the door and left in the cool wind.

His mother pinched Mark's cheeks, hard. "You need to follow him. He'll listen to you."

He pretended not to hear her.

She said, "Make sure he doesn't do anything crazy like walk off the rim."

"Why would he want to do that?"

She didn't answer, so he draped on his cape and crept after his father from a distance. He was discreet the way his mother told him to be, but it wouldn't have mattered—his father didn't notice anything. His father sat on a bench gleaming with dampness and counted the number of stars out loud to himself. When a couple walking by stared at him as if he were crazy, Mark felt protective.

He looked comfortable, no longer intently studying people, no longer ill at ease. He could not imagine his father as a kid playing soccer or having kid friends in North Korea, the land of missiles and rogue leaders in newspapers. His father got up and pulled wide the elastic band of his sports sock and withdrew a bill. He walked to a small shopping center and into a bakery, and a few minutes later appeared with a white box. Mark followed several yards behind. They walked. Away from the stores and restaurants, away from the streetlights, away from the motel, away from what seemed everything he had ever known. He wondered if they were going to walk all night. There were so many stars that he wanted badly to name all the constellations out loud and impress his father. He missed his father.

His father walked, beaming a flashlight ahead of him, and Mark tiptoed behind him, to the rim. They were standing on forty layers of limestone, sandstone, and shale. It felt like they were at the edge of the world. His father leaned against the flimsy wire fence and kicked a stone over the crumbly ledge. They both leaned forward, son behind the father, listening for the sound of the stone, but there was only the wind. It was a long way down and he was sure that every year there were accidents, the kind that couldn't be undone. Mark was afraid, seeing his father at such a vulnerable place, the cake box pressed to his chest and one foot raised knee-high as if to climb the fence. He prepared to tackle his father like a common athlete and endanger his velvet cape if necessary, anything to stop him from doing *the awful thing*. His father stepped forward; Mark squatted a few yards back, about to spring into NFL action, but his father sat in the dirt and opened the box. Inside there was a scalloped cake that he studded with candles.

Mark realized that it was past dinnertime; his mother would have a lukewarm but delicious dinner waiting for them.

"Happy birthday to you," his father sang, his hands over the candlelit cake as if it were a cozy fireplace.

Mark was weak with relief. His father was a reasonable man, a man who knew not to test the gravitational laws of the universe. He knew to go only when it was his time. It was the father he knew, using inscrutable ways of getting at something, but still Mark cried, his knuckle in his mouth so that the crying was happening in some other dimension and time, because he was a boy and boys did not cry.

Soon everything was quiet and he was no longer shaking. He and his father watched the emptiness of the canyon below, and the sky above that was a dense blanket of stars. It was the kind of silence that allowed the voices of the wind to be heard as they moved above, across, along the bottom of the canyon, where the bones of explorers must be buried. It was enough to make him want to write a poem, though poetry was for girls.

Only when his father cut a slice of cake, a frosted masterpiece the size of a travel-size chessboard, and lobbed it over the rim as if feeding the canyon, only then did Mark find the courage to speak.

"Don't waste cake!" he said. "Think of the poor kids in North Korea. Think of me."

His father smiled. The most awful smile Mark had ever witnessed.

"That was for Big Uncle who you never met," he said. "It's his birthday today."

Mark wondered if his father threw away a cake every year. He said, "You scared me, Appa."

"Never be scared of me," he said. He had the blank look of someone not present, and this made Mark angry at the past that kept taking his father away from him.

Mark vowed that he would never allow anything bad to happen to himself; he would hurtle into the present, straight into a large two-story house, and live in the same neighborhood into his white-whiskered age, install his parents as his neighbors, and raise a litter of gifted children with Chanhee. There would be no disasters or loss, nothing unplanned. He was carefully navigating the future when his father surprised him with a hug—if you could call it a hug. It was more like a slow-motion tackle that squeezed out the thin stream of air in Mark's windpipe and left him breathless, and with a longing he did not understand. He was overwhelmed.

"Mani sarang handa," his father said. I love you so much.

His arms enfolded Mark like warm bathwater, and stayed tight around his neck and shoulders. "Appa, I can't breathe," he said, but his father did not let go.

THE PASTOR'S SON

M Y MOTHER'S LAST wish was to have my father marry a childhood friend of hers: Hyeseon Min. Hyeseon had lived with her parents in Seoul her entire life, supported herself by giving piano lessons to rich children, and, as we learned later, read romance novels and the Bible with equal interest. Love wasn't mentioned; sex wasn't imagined. At that time, everyone, even I, naively believed that Hyeseon desired a kind of insurance in her old age—nothing more, because that was what she promised my mother.

But when we left California and its memories in December, and arrived for the wedding in Seoul, Hyeseon had blushed as she gripped my father's hands to her like a twenty-year-old. It was embarrassing for my sisters and me, and mortifying for my father to endure. Instead of the promised quiet family gathering, Hyeseon's tribe had opted for a typical Korean ceremony and hired a flashy wedding hall for several hundred acquaintances. Our recently widowed father was forced to ride a mechanized

Venetian gondola to the altar; a fog machine blew smoke into his face, and we endured two wedding ceremonies: a Western-style ceremony followed by a private Korean *pyebaek,* where nine dates and chestnuts were tossed into the skirt of Hyeseon's *hanbok,* which meant that she would have nine children.

"Pastor Ryu, tonight's the night," said one man to my father with a wink, as Hyeseon lurched around with a tiara perched on her perm.

I watched my father, his muscular body barely contained in the funereal black suit and his white pastor's collar that he had worn for fifteen years, the span of my life at the time. He made a stately matron blush to her fingertips, then bear-hugged her stolid husband, and I was surprised as I always was by his charisma. How easily it fooled people.

He was the only parent I had left and I wanted to believe that the marriage would save him. And I had almost convinced myself, right up until New Mother finished waving at guests like a celebrity, and hitched her froth of pink and white and entered the hired sedan.

As soon as he drove past the hotel entrance, my father stopped and flung his corsage in her face.

He said, "All your lies about a small family wedding were heard straight in heaven."

New Mother touched her cheek with the rose petals as if my father had stroked her. Her fingers dreamily scaled up and down the dashboard as if it were a piano.

My oldest sister covered my eyes, but I wasn't a child anymore, so I pulled away from her. I said, "Abeoji, we're holding up a parade of cars."

My father turned to the backseat and grabbed my arm so tight, the skin bubbled up around his fingers. "Son, I'd rather not hear from you right now," he said.

One of my older sisters scrambled out of the car, her hands to her throat in an asthma flare-up. In her rush she tore her silk dress on her heel, but leaning outside against the car window, her aspirator in her mouth, she didn't care. Only then I realized that my life was changed forever. I wouldn't live in the same time zone as my friends in America, I could never go to the record store and have long, meaningless conversations with the salesclerk about the reason why everyone should buy a copy of the new Culture Club CD, and my two older sisters would soon rejoin their good-hearted, steady Jewish husbands in Jersey City, and leave me alone in Korea with my father and the stranger I was supposed to call New Mother.

"My doctor," New Mother said, "says it may not be too late to have children."

She was fifty.

My father's head fell against the wheel as if he were exhausted. The horn blared long; New Mother didn't flinch. Her eyes were luminous; her wide gummy smile ardent with worship. I found myself sympathizing with New Mother in spite of myself.

Six months into the marriage my life had changed. I had come into school in the middle of the term and hadn't made a single friend. They treated me like a foreigner, saying I spoke Korean like a fourth grader, even getting angry when I answered questions in English class. They said I showed off about my life overseas because I talked about myself too much. No one talked much to me or to a Japanese girl who cried each time a student told her that her country had colonized Korea. I pretended I didn't care. Instead I spent all my time running and studying Korean comic books, dreaming about blowing up everyone at my new school, trying not to think about my mother.

Home was no better. One Saturday at noon, the day of my father's sixtieth birthday celebration, I found him asleep in his white briefs, sprawled underneath our last family portrait taken before my mother died. The picture was one of the only reminders of the dozen American cities of my childhood. Like many Koreans living overseas at the time, we had scraped by, living without the health insurance we couldn't afford, without security, and after my mother's hospital bills came in, we lost the little we had. Bankrupt and determined to honor my mother's last wishes, my father decided that marrying her childhood friend in Seoul had become his only option.

The marriage had only made him worse. The sixtieth birthday was a day as celebrated as weddings, but my father, who had spent his entire church life guarding his reputation, was now flat on the floor. He had a mane of ageless black hair swept to his street fighter's shoulders (much later, I realized it was dyed), a face marked by time and travel and adversity, the weary smile of Job. During the postwar years, he had been a shoe shiner, a hustler, a whaler, and then a *kkangpae,* that part of his life still evident in the speckled orange-and-white carp and goblins tattooed across the barrel of his chest and swimming up his spine. And after these many lives, when he had no one and nowhere to go, he had turned to God. He who had once shaken chapels and made the figure on the wooden cross weep, attracted disillusioned millionaires, exiled

Korean divorcées, dancers, and Christian zealots across America's prairie lands and its desert communities, this man who had once been so mighty behind the pulpit, whose rod and staff I worshipped, feared, and hated, had become so weak, so human in scale, he reminded me of myself.

"Son." His voice struck me like a fist. He rocked to his side and held an empty *soju* bottle to his eye. "Where is my heaven?"

"Abeoji." I backed away. "Drinking like you do, you'll lose your way to heaven."

He hooked my ankle with his foot and tripped me, then laughed when I fell.

"Adeul-ah." His head sagged. He stared at the bottles surrounding him as if they were a message from God. "Funny how I keep talking and talking but no one seems to answer. I can't sleep because I can't see her . . . She was my Ruth, my Esther, my Mary."

He stood up, his head nearly touching the ceiling, a permanent dampness above us, as if the basement home—more a cave than a home—had been a sponge for cycles of wet monsoon summers. He wobbled over to New Mother's potted begonia, adjusted himself, then peed on the plant. The sound of the spraying was a stunted dribble, a waterfall in dry season.

"She's gone," he said as he dried himself on a leaf. "Everyone's gone."

"I'm here," I said. "And New Mother's making lunch."

"Everyone leaves me, eventually," he said. He looked through me, his eyes dark and full with his absent family: my mother and his daughters; his mother, brothers, and sisters trapped north of the 38th parallel since 1953, when America and Russia carved up the country and left my father stranded in the south, where he had been volunteering, against his family's wishes, in the joint U.S.-Korean forces.

He wanted my sympathy, but I was young, angry at him, angry at God, in a country that didn't feel like mine, living with a man I thought I didn't love. I wanted to be part of a house where the father wasn't king and his kids the subjects, to be a boy whose stomach wasn't always knotted up, afraid each word he said was the wrong word. I wanted to be like my American friends, to be Gary, who called his professor father "Dad" and so naturally, so democratically, argued with him about who should be the next U.S. president. I wanted my mother, who was gone forever, no matter what they told me at church.

"Abeoji," I said. "Let's be objective here. No one made you remarry."

He looked at me as if he couldn't understand what I was saying. But the ardor of his gaze, that vast and lonely seeking, couldn't immobilize me anymore; it no longer impressed me how he would hit his children, then after, pull out strands of his own hair and butt his head against the walls until he bled, angry at his sins. So I walked away from him only a little afraid, because I was no longer the boy who confused his father with God.

It was past one before we sat as a family for lunch. We could see the feet of passersby through a barred window. New Mother had upgraded this subterranean life of ours with a lace tablecloth and silver candlesticks arranged over the piano bench; she had insisted on a grand piano, which meant in this space, there was no dining table or even a low *saang*. All the while my real mother gazed down at the new us.

I blessed the food, my sisters overseas. Before I finished, my father uttered "Amen," then slurped kelp soup from one of New Mother's flowery china bowls. With his chopsticks halfway to his mouth, he fell asleep, dropping a cube of steaming tofu into his lap.

New Mother poked her finger deep into his ear. "That's what you get for drinking the night long!" she said, as if he hadn't done the same thing throughout their short marriage.

She wiped his mouth with a napkin. One hundred percent linen, she proudly informed us. New Mother had brought these things, and more, into the marriage. Most of all, she had brought with her a faith in new beginnings. While we ate, her feet tapped staccato notes, her fingers waltzed across the table, her head danced left and right as she tried to convince us—even Mother's portrait, it seemed—that all was well. She turned her heavy breasts in my direction. There were too many teeth in her smile and her green pantsuit was a size too small, so I saw more than I wanted to. God, my father liked to say, had punished New Mother with her face.

She said, "Jingyu, did you make nice friends yet?"

"School's one long vocabulary lesson," I said. I missed America, the two dark, chain-smoking, antisocial friends I'd make in every city we moved to when my father grew restless, the anonymity.

"You should set yourself to memorizing a hundred new words a day." She clapped her hands, straining to be helpful. "I'll make you memory cards! In my student days, our *hakwon* teachers beat us unless we learned three hundred each day."

"I don't want to learn." I picked the black beans out of my rice, which she frowned at. "I want to go home."

"Home, home . . ." my father said. "Even Odysseus longed for home." He hacked up a globule of phlegm, spit it into the linen napkin, and folded it up.

New Mother blinked. Her pointy nose flared, but she focused on me as if nothing had happened. "Jingyu, women like men who have good posture; it makes you look taller. And you should smile more often—we'll get that tooth fixed one of these days."

My father had knocked out that tooth when I was eleven, but that was a family secret.

"Leave my son alone," my father said. His voice rattled the chopsticks. "He's not from your bloodline anyways. Old women like you get to a certain age and think too much. Only God knows what moves in the heart."

"He spends half his waking hours hiding in his room, sleeping and reading his mother's old Bible. If you took interest in anyone but yourself—"

"I am interested." His voice was clipped, dangerous. "Just not interested in you."

She flashed a large, unnatural smile that made her look more wounded than cheerful. "It's my money," she said. "Don't forget."

"Can't we just eat like other families?" I said.

"Is this a family?" He turned toward me, his hands gripping the bench by both sides. "Where is my family?"

In the late afternoon at my father's *hwanggap,* the guests parted like the Red Sea as he made his way down the hotel's ballroom, a playground for the rich that he had insisted on renting. He contemplated his guests with a studied pastor's modesty. As the emcee lauded my father's piety with limp anecdotes, my father timed his entrance from behind the towering cylinders of nuts, dates, fruits, and rice cakes that would be wheeled out again the next day for the next *hwanggap* party.

"Friends." He leaned across the podium as soon as the emcee fell silent. The gaudy silk screen of swooping cranes and lotus flowers made his eyes blacker. He paused, lifting his head slowly as if fatigued, and I wondered if this time he wouldn't be able to perform. Then he began.

"What it means to be back after all these years away. Some of you I haven't been privileged to see for twenty years, but none of you have forgotten Seoul's prodigal son. No matter how far I strayed, the good Lord does not forsake His children; He did not let me know the darkness of being a sheep without a shepherd for longer than I can bear." His voice broke, and his hands swept across his eyes, but he continued. He outstretched his hands and embraced the audience. "Jesus laid down his life for the sheep, so that we, the blind, would not be exiled from the Lord."

"Yaesu," someone said, calling out the name of Jesus.

"Oh, Juyeo," someone said even louder.

"Yaesu-nim," someone said, louder still.

"But even Jesus prayed into the night. Like Jesus who knew what it meant to suffer, our hearts must muse and our spirits must inquire, until the miracle happens."

He looked confusedly at the audience, as if he had forgotten that he was not at church, and that they were not his congregation. Then he recovered and said, "Now, it is another miracle to see so many decades of lives, so many generations here facing me, a miracle made true by God."

He spoke of the time our family had spent overseas, my mother's death, and especially the ministry that he said had saved him and made him better than he was. Finally he gestured to us.

"My busy daughters are married and working in America, but there they are, my son and his new mother."

When we stood and bowed, he beamed. New Mother's face lit up like a votive candle. From looking at them, you wouldn't think that each believed their life ruined by the other.

He began to pray, his voice thundering in the quiet hall. It was a voice that as a kid I used to mistake for God's. The entire chandeliered hall rang as his voice led us to the promised land, and for the length of that prayer, even skeptics must have believed. But when I opened my eyes, the certainty in his voice didn't match his face. His eyes were shut, his face tight and seeking, as if he had lost his way. I didn't want to see my father like this. I didn't look again.

When the prayer ended, he made his way down the hall, greeting women in ruffled blouses and men in gray-checked suits with his hands clasped around theirs; he anointed with his touch the heads of children scrambling between their mothers' skirts and the tablecloth; he kissed the wasted cheeks of women who had been wheeled out from nursing homes; he embraced the people whom he had reunited with in the past six months in Seoul: CEOs, factory workers, gang members, professional *pansori* singers in horsehair hats, a dizzy number of church people. He forgot no one. But when he sat between New Mother and me, our dwindled family, he seemed to shrink.

Middle-aged women in pastel suits pushed around the buffet tables heavy with sweet fried pork; salted mackerel; chunks of beef soaked in soy sauce and honey, and garnished with gingko nuts; crispy tofu; cold jellyfish salad; abalone porridge; raw fish and squirming baby squid; a dozen fermented vegetables and wild roots. Older women with hands like cigarette paper stroked my cheek.

"He's a goldfish copy of his mother," they said.

Each time, I made my greeting and darted away.

A silver-haired man in a plaid suit and oxfords said, "I think of your mother all the time."

But I wasn't ready to talk to strangers about my mother. I wasn't about to tell them how her hair had grown in coarse and gray, how I had circled the block several times after school before facing her relentless pain, the moans that ground into my every thought until I never wanted to think again, or how she had begged me to put her to sleep as the morphine reached toxic levels without easing the pain, and that wasn't the worst of it. It must have been the same for my father, though he thanked the man for his kind words. New Mother, who overheard, started tapping that foot of hers.

The men concentrated on eating. These men who had grown up in wartime didn't let conversation interrupt. As the saying goes, they wouldn't have noticed even if someone at the table had died. They swallowed in hurried, dogged silence; they knew the value of food. In the rest of the hall, men drank and complained about jobs; women bragged about their children while wrapping extra food in the hotel's napkins, some even brought Tupperware and plastic bags; others sang and danced to a rented karaoke machine, changing the cassette tape each time the music ran out; kids my age roamed around the hall as bored as I was; others passed out business cards. At our table, the conversation inevitably turned to God.

A man with a bushy monobrow said that the church needed to prepare for the future of North Korea. "Just think about all those unsaved souls in Pyongyang alone. It makes me want to get on my knees and pray."

"Basic needs first," my father's voice barreled down the table. "Those people suffer; they're still living the war. Give them democracy, and meat, first."

"Prayer is our food," said the man with a nose like a fishhook. "Next you'll be saying that Jesus and Buddha are brothers."

"Ah," New Mother said. "There's a thrilling book on just that subject."

As if these men stuck in another era were interested in a woman's opinion, she began talking. Even I, who didn't think of myself as a real Korean, knew my place. She jabbed her fork at the centerpiece of roses while she made her point. "As early as 1979—"

"Why don't each of you stand up and say something nice about me?" my father said. His voice was needy. I slipped lower into my seat, ready for the evening to be over.

"Pastor Ryu saved my life, in the army," said the eyebrow. "You could've left me on the field." His lips trembled. "But you took me out of there on your back."

New Mother's head jerked up obstinately. "I was saying—"

"This man loaned me money when my own family turned me out," said another. "No questions, nothing. Like a brother. Better than a brother." He embraced my father. "You are my brother."

The stories kept coming, some that I knew, many that I'd

never heard because my father rarely talked about his past. He kept his eyes turned above the crowd to the frosted cupcake of a ceiling. His face was greedy, insecure, solitary. New Mother was biting down on her fingernails; I could see her thinking that if she were my mother, Father would have let her finish her sentence. The sad fact is my mother would have gone into a cave of quiet, with opinions and feelings I only wondered about once she was gone. Long before any of us were born, it seemed, she had given up hope of changing a thousand years of tradition, or my father.

"Look at my boy eat."

My father patted me. The entire table looked over as I popped a piece of fried pork in my mouth.

"He's all appetite. He stays skinny like that because all he does is run. You did twenty kilometers this afternoon, didn't you, Jingyu? In the rain, too."

I shrugged.

My father sighed. "He reminds me of me."

His friends disagreed.

"No, he's more like his mother's body, long and lean."

"Well, he's got your bones, but he's too pretty to look like you."

"You're one of those quiet but notice everything types, aren't you?" said a man with a dribble of soy sauce down his chin. "Your mother was like that, a rare woman. That's a wise way to be. People shouldn't waste words."

New Mother's heel tapped harder under the table. It got so the silverware rattled. The conversation continued to swirl around and past her. She picked at a mound of glass noodles, her face absurd, mournful. When the men happy with *soju* began toasting one another, she pushed back her chair so quickly, it caught the tablecloth and sent her silverware crashing to the floor. She weaved out of the hall, her face volcanic with misery. Abeoji laughed.

"Just like a woman," he said.

She was probably looking for a piano somewhere in the hotel. You couldn't really blame her—the room was filled with the past, and Mother's ghost seemed everywhere. It was too much, even for me.

"I can't compete with a dead person." New Mother slapped at her palm. Within minutes of coming home she had begun listing her grievances.

"Be quiet, woman."

My father shoved the piano bench at her. When it hit the side of her knee, she fell.

He said, "You've humiliated me enough."

"Let's get some rest," I said.

She rose shaking, her bad leg floundering behind her. She took the picture of my mother off the wall and held it like a shield.

"That's not for you to touch," I said. I grabbed for it, but she hugged it to her chest.

My father punched the piano keys, all dissonant notes.

"Getting you to listen is like reading the Bible to a cow," he said.

"A new start's overdue for everyone."

"It's been a year, only one year, since your best friend died."

"I'm a woman. A woman."

"You told her you wanted marriage as life insurance, nothing more from me. Put the picture where it belongs, you middle-aged virgin."

She began to cry. I stood between my father and her, wanting to walk out, wanting to be anywhere but here, but her fear kept me suspended. I knew that fear well.

"I'll break the picture." She held it high in the air. My mother, still young, still healthy, gazed hopefully out of the frame. "I swear I'll break it."

"She pitied you." His voice thrummed with pleasure.

New Mother hurled the picture across the room.

The frame crashed to the floor, and glass struck out everywhere. With the last shards still tinkling, I scrambled to my knees and started picking up torn pieces of the picture. I didn't care if I was a boy; there was a piece of my mother's arm in my right hand, a shred of her nose in my left, and I was crying for my mother.

My father seized New Mother by her hair and hauled her to the floor.

Still, she didn't beg to be forgiven. Instead she said, "No one knows who you are, but God knows!"

I was still angry and didn't step between them when he dragged her out the door.

My mother's image was too broken up. There was nothing left of her now. She was gone. What was left in the house was the meager life that the years had given her, the smell of a man who had terrified her into becoming invisible. There were my sisters who had married men they knew they could dominate if needed, and me, unable to speak to people because anything that felt true about me was a secret.

Then I left the house.

I ran until I caught sight of them, and followed them from a ways back, calling to my father. But near the Han River walkway, I lost the two in the fog. I checked the parking lot, my hands feeling out before me. The rain swallowed the silence. The pleasure boat was docked, the paddleboats empty. One minute the rain thinned, then a sheet of rain fell so thick it erased my hands.

It must have been ten yards ahead on the riverside walk. I was straining to see when I spotted my father thrusting New Mother into the river water. Closer, enormous bubbles—her ragged breathing—rose up from the water. When he yanked her back up, New Mother's breasts sagged out of her unknotted *choguri,* the skirt of her *hanbok* stuck to her heavy thighs. Her moan was like the sound of whales spuming. When he clawed off her hands, her body keeled over as he released her into the water.

I shouted, "I'll get the police! I will!"

He thrust her in and out. There was no struggle now, no breath of resistance, nothing in that body except for her small exhausted sounds.

I scrambled down the embankment to the river's edge. I was nearly on top of them, but he didn't stop. Only then I locked him by his arms and hauled him off her.

He looked at me, his eyes black with anger. He said, "Go home, *jashik.* There's no happiness here."

New Mother's flattened curls shrouded her face. She crouched on the cement, her breathing uneven.

I said, "Stop it, please. God is everywhere . . ."

He looked crazed, sad. He gripped himself, trying to contain himself. But then he was on me. His breath was hard on my cheek as he locked me from behind by my arms.

"Decades my junior and you think you have rights? You think we're American?"

His teeth scraped against my ear.

"You're no *baekin* from America with white skin. You look like me."

I laughed, convinced there was nothing of my father in me.

"On your knees," he said. "And I want real sorrow in that apology. Say it."

New Mother said, "He's your boy." She flinched with fear at her own words.

"You." He pointed through the fog to the ghostly cars. "Go away, woman. Leave my family alone."

His eyes bore into her.

I told her, "Go! This isn't about you."

Finally she began walking backward, away from us, her eyes on him the entire time. "I'm getting help, don't worry!" She kept screaming this until she was no longer there.

He squatted, his shoulders like a *ssireum* wrestler's, his legs spidery. "I'll break your legs if you don't get down on them yourself."

"Is this the only way, Abeoji, hurting people?"

"Who are you, telling your father what he is and what he isn't? You *mot-nan gaesaekki*!"

His voice rammed into me, he swore he would teach me.

His fist struck me in the stomach; his leg reared back. I heard a snap—like ice cracking in spring—as I fell. When the foot kicked out again, I balled up, my arms around my skull, and waited for the blows from my father, the man I should love. I tried to imagine myself somewhere else, someone else, but I only saw myself on the cold pavement. I was young, a stranger in my own country, again my father's easy victim.

His foot sailed out again; I did the unforgivable. That foot, my father's own foot, I caught with one hand. Then I hit him.

He lay on the pavement. His lips were parted as if he were thirsty. The rain beat down on his face, his nose bled, and his forehead swelled a dull purple. He closed his mouth, opened it. He was trying to say something.

"Jingyu, I don't know why—this anger—" He looked up. "Jingyu, don't cry. Please."

He kissed my head, my chest. His hands were wet, rubbery, as he caressed my hand. I saw he didn't want me to leave him, like all the others had.

"You know what I think about every day?" I said. "I ask myself why God took the wrong parent."

My father dragged himself up, his hair shiny against his forehead. I listened, unmoved by his weary breaths. "You know the old saying?" he said. "If your parents die, you bury them in the mountains. If your child dies, you bury him in your heart." He reached for me the way he always did when he was calmer. "Adeul-ah, no one will ever love you the way I do."

"What do you want from me?"

The rain came. My father sighed, the sound threadbare, labored.

"Jingyu, I didn't have a father," he said. "I don't know how to be a father."

I stood still. He paced, then turned back. His brogues made prints in the rain before they were washed away.

"This rage . . ." His voice slowed. "I can't slow myself—"

"Enough, Abeoji."

I walked away. When I held my hands out in front of me, they were shaking. They were strangers to me, these large knuckles and thick fingers I would grow into. I turned.

"Adeul-ah . . ."

I said nothing.

My father took off his shoes and laid them neatly on the cement as if he had just come home. He sat, legs folded over each other, then got up again, as if he wasn't sure where he wanted to be. He walked over. His hands held my face, and he stared deep into my eyes. He kissed my cheeks.

"Adeul-ah, pray for me." His voice dropped. "No matter what, tell them I drowned."

And just as I moved toward him, my father turned his back on me and on God, and stepped casually off the riverside path and into the river.

I have not looked at photos of my father for years. His bloated river face and emptied-out eyes have faded for me, though I still hear his cadences, those broken incantations that rang through my childhood. Soon after my father's passing, I stopped attending church. No matter how often New Mother reminded me that I was a pastor's son, I could never go back.

During my college years I dutifully visited New Mother; sometimes I just made phone calls. Every year I poured the rice wine that my father liked so much over his grave and pulled the weeds around the tombstone; I ordered flowers for my mother's grave, stranded in America. Just after I graduated, I fell in love with and married a woman who nurtured the faith that I no longer could. Through her, even after we returned to America, a part of me stayed connected to Korea and to the church. I believed myself to be happy, or at least reconciled, as we settled in New Jersey, acquired our first mortgage, and took weeklong holidays in the summers and winters.

Time passed for me, time stayed still. Seoul is a city that, no matter its changes as it modernized, I will always remember as my father's. On my last day there, I walked through Woo Meat Market, where merchants unload pigs' heads leaking blood from the mouths and necks, and passed men staggering into the dark, men seeking brawls and seeking love. I saw the violence that my father had grown up with and passed down to us. I felt what my father must have always carried with him: the terrible war, its long-ago shadow that cast far beyond and drew you in like a thirsty curse. Only then I understood what the war had done to us.

When the monsoon rains descended that July, I thought of how he had wanted to walk with God but had been incapable of it. I see now that his slightly bowlegged walk is my walk; that my black, watchful eyes are his. When I see a stranger hunched over, devouring a cut of filet mignon as if it were a bowl of ramen, I see my father and the hunger he had grown up with. There he is for me, an orphan, hungry all his life.

THE GOOSE FATHER

Even after soonah and their two children had left Seoul for Boston, Gilho Pak denied that he was what the newspapers dubbed a "goose father," one of those men who faithfully sent money to his family living overseas. The original goose fathers, the term signifying their journey from one country to another, were Korean men who had been drafted or volunteered as mercenary soldiers for the U.S. army in Vietnam, and sent their salaries back to their family. But back then, there had been few jobs and a national landscape of poverty. Gilho was not a goose; he was entirely stationary. He was a successful accountant who did not associate himself with the Vietnam mercenaries, much less the so-called goose fathers reduced to eating ramen for dinner; those men so dishonest they had other women in their wives' absence, men who collapsed from strokes, unearthed in their homes weeks later by neighbors, men less than men in their solitude. Unlike those fathers, his family's absence made Gilho even more upright and correct in his behavior. Sex? He had never understood the fuss. And what about Junho, his ten-year-old son, and his daughter, Jinhee, in American private schools, his wife's language-school tuition that qualified her for a student visa, their living expenses? He'd had the foresight of a self-made man, and made sound investments before the country's financial crisis in 1998.

Still, despite the books he finally had time to read and the spotless flooring he could maintain, loneliness made him feel like a house teetering on an eroding cliff. He dreaded the evening quiet of his apartment, and resorted to making phone calls to friends as he moved from room to room that rebuked him with their emptiness. The night he woke up hugging his daughter's filthy baseball mitt, he decided to put a stop to this nonsense. So six months after separation from his family, he advertised, interviewed several candidates, then settled for a tenant, a boy who seemed as alone as Gilho.

The next week when Gilho came home, the tenant was sitting on the doormat. He had two suitcases stacked in front of him and a goose the size of an overfed house cat in his arms. A goose of all creatures, as if the boy was mocking Gilho. The bird shifted and revealed a splash of white paint across its dung-colored chest, as if God—though Gilho no longer believed in God—had slipped up with his paintbrush.

Gilho charged past the lanky boy and opened the door, but Wuseong scrambled to his feet and grasped his shoulder with his free hand. Gilho was about to dismiss him, call off their agreement, but he froze as he took in the boy's anxious rosebud lips, the drooping pine needle scar that marred his chin, his shaved monkish head. Somehow, despite the goose's grime, the boy managed to look so clean. He was almost too pretty to be a boy, Gilho thought before he escaped into the apartment.

At the threshold the boy hovered and looked helplessly into the museum-white living room, just as Gilho had twenty years earlier when he, a farmer's son from the island of Geoje, had been looking for cheap accommodations. He had been the first one in the family to attend college, and the first person in his village to be accepted by Seoul National University, the nation's most prestigious institution. His father had killed two pigs in Gilho's honor and held a party for the village, complete with a giant banner announcing his son's achievements. Gilho had been an earnest student afraid of failing his family, overwhelmed by gratitude when a wealthy, popular girl on campus, now his wife, began paying attention to him. But over the years, he had excised the farm boy, stamped out his provincial traces, and become used to this new him.

"This goose—you didn't mention a goose," Gilho said. "Do you know how many germs it carries? It'll infest my home."

"Pak *ajeoshi*." The boy's address for older men was as supple as fresh rice cakes. He clutched the goose to his gaunt chest, and his eyes opened wide in alarm. "Oh, you can't turn away a goose with only one good wing—she just found me! That's like Superman without his cape. Like General Yi Sun-shin without his Turtle Ship. I swear she'll be out of the way on the balcony."

Gilho had accepted a month's rent in advance. There was his balcony of horticultural treasures, but he was not a person to violate his commitments. He sank into the leather sofa.

"I advertise for a tenant; I get a dirty little bird."

Wuseong stroked the goose with long pianist's fingers. Like a tamed animal, the goose rested its head against the boy's thin chest. Then the boy scuttled over to the balcony, slid open the glass door, and deposited the goose in the middle of Gilho's plants. It stretched its short tuber neck and disappeared behind a waxy green frond. After waving to it, the boy hefted his suitcases up and deposited them in the spare room. He returned hunched, one tentative foot at a time, so different from the way Gilho had become: a man used to having his way, a man used to making demands.

"Please, Ajeoshi," Wuseong said. He blushed like a newlywed. "It's eight o'clock at night and we don't have anywhere to go."

They were an incongruous pair: a man whose gaze did not seem to take in anything more than it needed to; whose very walk was efficient and with purpose; the kind of man who seemed to have ambled out of his mother's womb fully formed. Wuseong teetered like a beanstalk when he walked; his speech hovered precariously between leisure and panic. He watched in awe as Gilho completed fifty push-ups while reading a newspaper spread flat on the ground.

Gilho stood up, his breathing even as if his body had been at rest.

Gilho said, "If that bird eats my plants, it's leaving first thing tomorrow morning."

"Goodnight, my *ajeoshi*."

Gilho shook his head, and turned away.

Precisely at six the next morning, Gilho headed to the balcony with a steaming mug of green tea. He cultivated, among other plants, cacti, specializing in Mexican Tehuacán desert specimens that he kept warm through the forbidding winters with a special heating unit. For a decade he had found refuge each morning in this forest of cacti, where, before facing the grayness of his responsibilities, he read out loud half a dozen *sijo,* three-line classical poems that made him shiver with their beauty. But when he slid open the glass door, the goose fixed its gelatinous eyes on him and honked. It was resting on a shelf next to a potted *Aloe bellatula.* Alarmed, he pumped his arms at the goose. One wing dragged crookedly as if broken, and the other, billowing like a dirty white parachute, struck him in the face.

Gilho fled from the bean goose, the mutt of all birds. He was a forty-six-year-old accountant, an age and a profession that in their society commanded respect. He had relinquished so many possible selves to rescue his children from Korea's university exam hell and his wife from the crippling anxiety of the education disease, and the boy dared taunt this so-called goose father with a goose; he deserved better than this mockery!

He hunted down Wuseong.

Wuseong was in the kitchen flipping a scallion pancake in the air. His motions were languid and confident; like all of them, a different person when he was alone. Seeing Wuseong with the washcloth perched on his head like a chef's hat, his singular pleasure in the browning edges of the pancake, made Gilho forget his anger.

"Surprise!" Wuseong said. "You haven't had a homemade meal for some time, I'm sure."

Since Soonah had left, Gilho had resorted to buying egg and toast or a roll of *kimbap* at vendors' stands; seeing the steaming food made him feel sentimental. It was also uncomfortable, seeing a man performing a woman's role.

"But—I don't have anything for you," he said.

"You can write me a poem!" Wuseong looked hopeful.

Gilho felt a phantom pain at the word. *Poem.* It had been years since anyone had talked about poems with him. He had belonged to the literature club on campus; some of those friends had become Korea's most exciting writers, but while they had risked and struggled, he had built himself a fortress of security and accepted the changes it had exacted from him.

"How did you know I write—wrote poetry? No one knows that about me."

The boy flipped the pancake once, twice, before saying, "I read your first book of poems."

"My only book of poems."

"Your only book of poems." He clasped his hands in a kind of prayer. "I looked and looked . . . why wasn't there a second?"

"I didn't have a second in me . . . there was only a first," he admitted. "So that's why you went and found me? To see what this old dinosaur who once wrote a few poems is doing these days?"

"Yes."

"Well, now you know. He's an accountant with a faraway family who reads more than he should."

"Ajeoshi, don't be angry." His hands fluttered, graceful and nervous. "Those poems carved me out."

Gilho wasn't angry, just ashamed.

Wuseong inhaled the strong perfume of fish and bean paste stew. "You should eat."

Gilho obliged and tried the typical family breakfast: the

stir-fried garlic stems and seasoned vegetables and roots were rich with flavor; the haddock was grilled to gold; the steaming communal pot of *dwenjang* stew had a complex base of anchovies, garlic, seaweed, and mushrooms that changed on the tongue with time. The food, doing what only good food was capable of, helped him relax.

Gilho set his chopsticks down. "You could open a restaurant." Wuseong giggled and touched two fingers to his lips.

"That will never happen. I despise people, but I like cooking for you."

Gilho turned away shyly. "I've never heard anything so strange."

"Well, I don't really hate *hate* people. I'm too melodramatic," Wuseong said, and smiled. "It's a character flaw. I have a lot of those."

He sat back delicately, as if afraid that his weight would break the chair. But only long enough to suck a grain of rice off his chopsticks before he leaped up again. He set aside a bowl of lettuce and seeds, stuck a plastic daisy into a leaf, then admired the effect. Gilho stared as the boy tiptoed to the balcony to feed the goose fresh lettuce and potato wedges; its orange-banded bill the size of a kid's trowel swooped down as if to kiss the boy's palm.

Watching the boy, Gilho felt a little dizzy. Wuseong belonged to no category of people that he recognized, and it disturbed Gilho's hard-won world order.

When Wuseong returned with the goose in one arm, Gilho pushed his chair back and snatched his briefcase, still chewing the last spoonful of rice. He said, "*Gomab-ne.* Breakfast was filling, but don't do this again."

The boy struggled to maintain his smile; Gilho halted. He had not meant to be unkind. At the interview, he had learned that the boy's mother had passed away with kidney failure; his father he had lost contact with years ago. There was only the goose.

He said, "I mean, I don't want to waste your time."

Wuseong brightened with shy pleasure; like a boy unused to kindness, he was so easy to please. He shouted thank you and leaned forward so dangerously that Gilho leaped back to escape the hug. The boy frantically waved his free hand in the air as if Gilho were embarking on a long journey.

Over the next month Gilho learned that Wuseong was not only a skilled cook and a tamer of wildlife, but also an accomplished photographer, a collector of useless, arcane facts, a three-time employee of the month at Lotteria Burgers, and an amateur director who had shot two above-average short films on a borrowed camcorder, each made for less than the price of a cup of coffee. But Wuseong's immoderate passions made him quick to panic. At night Gilho heard him making disturbed talk in his sleep, sometimes crying out, his voice lashing through the silence. He spent weeks painting miniature boxes, then threw them away. All his closest friends, he said, were in jail; Gilho did not ask him any more about this. Perhaps because of the chaos of his past life, Wuseong seemed to delight in Gilho's solidity. All that was ordinary about Gilho—chewing an apple twenty-five times with each bite, reading while blow-drying his hair—was for the boy admirable, mysterious. As for Gilho, he often found himself at work wondering at this boy who didn't disguise his uncertainty, his eagerness to please, his poverty, everything that Gilho had worked so hard to hide. It was as if the only thing he knew how to be was genuine.

One morning he walked in on Wuseong talking to the goose.

"He's shy, my *ajeoshi*," said the boy.

My *ajeoshi*. This time, the use of the possessive made Gilho flush. He said, "And now you know how to interpret goose talk?"

The boy became radiant. "She's not a goose, she's my mother."

"Your mother?"

He shook his head to laugh, but he stopped when the boy disappeared behind a jumping cholla cactus.

"And what exactly is your mother saying to you?"

"I'm still learning how to understand it myself."

"I start humoring you, bringing back home bags of chopped salad and sunflower seeds for the goose, and you start seeing your mother?"

The boy popped out from behind a swollen cluster of cactus spines. "She promised me she'd come back, and she did. That's what matters."

Gilho shook his head. He said, "No, it's not possible."

The boy's nervous hands ruffled the goose's muscle of a neck; it angled toward the boy, submitted to its caretaker.

Gilho embarked on an awkward conversation concerning the cycle of life and death. He tried to be as gentle as he knew how. God? Allah? Buddha? *Mudang*? Wuseong retreated to the corner of ferns. He told the boy that all religions were ancient tricks aimed at parting you from your money, as if the boy were twelve and not twenty-two. "I wish you were right, but this isn't the answer," Gilho concluded. "A goose is finally a goose, no matter what you want it to be."

The boy's large eyes emerged over the ferns, his expression quizzical and unconvinced. He merely said, "I'm going to make you believe."

"I believe in helping people," Gilho said. "In responsibility. In family. And our country. But this is only a goose!"

"You don't need to justify yourself." The boy smiled the kind of smile that made Gilho's face heat up. "You're saying this because you care about me. It makes me happy."

All he knew was that Wuseong did not leave him alone. After work or rehearsals on a comic adaptation of *Hamlet* (Gilho had not known that it was possible), the boy came directly home and flustered Gilho by skating around the kitchen with soapy sponges tied to his feet while chanting ancient Buddhist sutras on reincarnation, which forced Gilho to childishly cover his ears with his hands, though more often Gilho would spend an evening listening to Wuseong read out loud his favorite poems; the boy, to add to his prodigious talents, had a voice with the clear tenor of a church bell. Another time, Gilho came home and found Wuseong asleep, curled up on the hardwood floor without a pillow or blanket, and no *yo* underneath him, and when Gilho woke him up, the boy looked straight at him and said, "Everywhere I go, a road," before falling immediately back to sleep. The line reminded Gilho that he had, finally, lacked the courage to trust the person he had wanted to be; he walked away to recover from vertigo. When he spoke of the boy's strangeness to Soonah on the phone, she said reasonably (she was always reasonable), "Why don't you find another tenant?"

Gilho could only wonder. In a country where a university degree made you respectable, the boy had dropped out because he wasn't being taught anything. He had thespian ambitions; he raised crippled animals for fun. His idealism couldn't last. But what might have happened if Gilho had not married and scrambled to provide Soonah the life that she and her parents, that everyone, expected, if he had not been so susceptible to her fear of risk, of failure, of others' eyes, all fears that were his own?

Two months into the boy's stay, Gilho was persuaded to visit a local song room with Wuseong. He had come home to the boy weeping about a documentary on the fate of krill whales, and in distress, Gilho had offered to cheer him up.

The song room hall was lit with last year's Christmas lights.

"So you want a *baang* for the hour?" A woman leaned over the counter, outraging Gilho's aesthetics with her silicone monstrosities.

Wuseong nodded, knocking gently against Gilho as his body swayed to a silent music. He kept saying, "We're having so much fun," after the *soju* they'd shared at the drinking tent just before. Somehow this friendship with a boy half his age had become possible though people with two years' difference between them called each other "junior" or "senior" but rarely friends. But Wuseong had no barriers; he was too guileless, Gilho thought, too trusting, and he found himself worrying about how the world would hurt him.

They were assigned a room that smelled vaguely of gym socks. As soon as the door closed Wuseong zipped open his oversize backpack and withdrew the goose. He told Gilho not to worry because in this song room people did whatever they pleased, but Gilho worried because that was his nature. Still, they sang from the book of songs sticky with soft drinks they drank. Wuseong plucked a pink wig off the video seat and put it on; he shook the tambourine while cavorting on the red velour couch. Gilho sang a famous folk ballad and cheered when he received a score of 100 from the machine. Even the goose, Gilho hated to admit, seemed to lumber to the music. He was feeling free and almost bohemian when he went searching for a bathroom and a girl with a large satin bow in her hair slipped past him into a room of three men. Maybe if they had enough to drink they would go somewhere else and have sex that night, the four of them.

He returned, quieter. Wuseong had lain down across the couch with his legs propped up, his face pink from the rushing blood. When he saw Gilho, he blew him a kiss.

Gilho said, "You really don't care what people think about you, do you?"

Wuseong considered this. "Not really, no."

"I've always cared about the good opinion of others," Gilho said. He had once been proud of this.

"What's wrong with that?" Wuseong sat upright. "You have people who care about your opinions."

He stared at the boy's calloused hands. When Wuseong straightened, Gilho looked up at his face, at the scar, which, he had begun to suspect, could also be the work of a blade. The face was young and willful, it was tired out with what it had seen. It made you want to believe. He found himself staring at the rosy flesh of the boy's lips as Wuseong leaned in, his face inching closer to Gilho's. Gilho shuddered, imagined his lips against Wuseong's lips. He slapped the boy instead.

Wuseong staggered backward, his hand cupping his cheek. Gilho's chest tightened like the beginning of a heart attack. A terrible loneliness spiked through him as he looked at the boy.

"Who are you?" said Gilho. "What are you doing to my life?"

Wuseong bowed repeatedly in apology. An elephantine tear slid down the slant of his cheek. Gilho's heart exploded with language, but he was locked into silence, searching for words, when Wuseong scooped up the goose and leaped away and out of the *noraebaang,* as graceful as a bird taking flight.

At work the next morning, Wuseong's alarm, the shadow of Gilho's palm across his face, haunted Gilho. He composed excuses for his behavior on company letterhead, then an hour later fed the pages into a paper shredder. He thought of his wife and children. Once he completed the half day's accounts, he hurried home. By the time he unlocked the front door he had convinced himself that nothing had happened, which was not difficult; raised in a media and around conversations where such feelings did not officially exist, he could not fathom them. But when he discovered that Wuseong had disappeared, goose in tow, Gilho sat watching the empty veranda until the sun came up.

He called in sick for the first time in his working life. He trudged through December's first snow, a stickiness that turned to slush as it hit the pavement, past the homeless camped inside Seoul Station, past the wealthy clientele—Soonah's people—on gallery row near Gyeongbokgung Palace, past a platoon of soldiers, mostly college boys fulfilling compulsory military service, surrounding the U.S. embassy, past the shivering applicants queued up all day for elusive American visas, as wind cut through his long underwear, disturbed his hair, and left him disoriented. On impulse he snuck into the nearest broker's office.

The manager with a bald spot the size of a dessert plate pulled out laminated charts. As he directed Gilho's attention to a graph with a laser beam he whipped out from his velvet jacket, Gilho thought of Soonah, their children, and the 457 days that he had spent without them. Business-investment visa, skilled-worker visa, education visa, visas, visas.

"You're lucky!" the man said, though Gilho did not feel lucky. "With your background you have so many options."

After the consultation Gilho signed the contract. For a green card, for escape, he was prepared to sell the apartment and stocks to reinvest in a country already fat on the world's wealth. Only then he saw too clearly how it would be: he would be a stuttering dwarf in a land of blond giants; he would arm himself behind a liquor store counter for the rest of his days. He would lie next to his wife, a stranger forever to him. This was no true escape. As Gilho ripped up the contract, he thought of the goose in its glassed-in balcony, ferociously defending its little bit of space.

He walked through the forest of skyscrapers into the slums of Chongyecheon, where shopkeepers weaved through traffic on bicycles and peddlers sold domestic porn films that showed little more than a mosaic of faceless body parts. Later, behind the Chongryangri Lotte Department Store, two prostitutes in Technicolor halter tops dashed out of their window displays and began their sales pitch. While peering left and right for the indifferent police (there had been yet another theoretical crackdown), he picked the one with long, straight hair, long legs, a little baby fat. He kept his hands firmly cupped around her pear-shaped breasts, but each time he blinked, the curve of her waist became a boy's hips. When she asked in a stale voice, "What is it about me, Ajeoshi?" he could not tell her the truth. Her eyes reminded him of Wuseong's.

On Wednesday Wuseong still had not returned. Gilho called the police on Thursday and found himself repeating to the impatient policeman that the boy was memorable. On Friday, after struggling with the tidy figures scrolling down his work monitor, he arrived late for his college alumni gathering in Yeoido. His friend Taeyeong greeted him with a slap on the shoulder and said, "I thought the goose got you."

Gilho almost left the barbecue restaurant, but only squeezed his friend's shoulder as he sat down.

They took turns pouring one another's shot glasses with the clear rice whiskey they had drunk together for over twenty years. They were all born in the same year, 1960, so they could speak *ban-mal* to one another, they could be comfortable together.

"Geombe!" they said.

"One shot!" a friend named Duik shouted, so they clicked their glasses, downed their drinks, then held the glasses upside down over their heads to show that they were empty.

They ate small chunks of roasted pork straight off the charcoal grill with garlic and wrapped in lettuce leaves. The owner's caged-up pet pig looked on. Gilho wondered briefly if it could smell the flesh of its own kind. He had been to this restaurant several times, but he hadn't considered the pig before. This perspective, he thought, was also what Wuseong opened up in him.

Jonghun to his right poured him beer mixed with *soju*.

"Friend, it's too early to drink *poktan-ju*," Gilho said. "We haven't even gotten to our second bar!"

But you should never refuse a drink from a friend, so he accepted the glass.

They were drinking; they were happily forgetting; they were slowly reaching the stage when they were no longer individuals and more like members of a group; the *uri*, the we in which everything dissolved: Duik's mother's death, Gilho's and Taeyeong's departed families, Sangwon's hostile marriage, Minjun's fragile solvency.

As the men drank, what seemed like a world of young people drifted past the large windows; at the next table a group of university students drank, still able to do anything and go anywhere, or become anyone.

Duik sighed. "Remember when we couldn't pay the bill and they hauled us to the police station—what was it, five in the morning?"

"Or when we ran out of money and walked six kilometers back home?"

"That was nothing compared with military service. They would keep us awake five days in a row—"

"For me it was a week."

"They'd give us a tiny bowl of water in the middle of summer after we'd run fifteen miles, and tell us to wash with it."

"Everyone was so thirsty we'd fight to drink water from the toilets."

"Now they get real food and cry when their squadron leader hits them."

"Koreans need to be beat."

"If they don't get beat, nothing gets done."

"They say the young kids these days get in taxis and run away without paying. Young people these days, they have no *ui-ri.* They've got no honor."

And yet they envied the young.

Within another hour, as was the custom, they moved to a bar for *icha,* the second round. Duik, his hair a glacial white since he'd turned thirty, stood up and sang into an empty *soju* bottle. Minjun picked through all the vegetables and ate only the chunks of cod in the spicy fish egg stew until another whacked him across the head.

When they talked about women, Gilho become quiet; when they'd had enough *soju,* they scrutinized their server's breasts.

Taeyeong said, "It's like visiting a brothel without paying for it."

His voice was merry, but his face wore the cost of two years' separation from his family.

Gilho looked up, his face bleak.

Taeyeong gripped his hand in mistaken sympathy. His wife and children had also left for America; he, too, understood what sacrifices it took to free your children from the sixteen hours of mindless daily cramming at school and after-school institutes that ran past midnight, the special Oriental medicines to keep them awake for college entrance exam studies, the temptation of suicide. But Gilho had been avoiding Soonah's calls for the past week.

The men kissed one another on the cheeks, their hands across one another's shoulders and backs. Taeyeong said, "My *chingu,*" and kissed Gilho on the lips. They had attended boys' schools, served in the military, and worked in corporations run like the army; they were more at ease around men. They were friends, they were men with *ui-ri,* loyal, steadfast men, and for their generation, that meant that they would underwrite one another's debts if asked, they would die for one another if needed.

Minjun, who had been sleeping with his head on the table for the last half hour, rubbed his eyes, yawned, and stood up on his chair.

"I love you. I love you all," he said, striking a skiing pose though they all knew he could not afford the sport. "I want to love you guys, so you better let me get the bill," he said.

While they fought with one another to pay, the piece of paper snatched from hand to hand, Taeyeong, who was a lawyer, quietly stood up and paid for them all.

That night, after the last round of drinks at a drinking tent, Gilho returned home after four with Taeyeong draped over him like an overcoat. He rested his friend on the couch, then slid to the floor. It was then that he saw Wuseong on the balcony. When their eyes met, the goose tucked its hammer-shaped head underneath Wuseong's neck and made a rough, throaty sound.

Gilho slid the balcony glass door open. *"Ah-yah,"* he said, "where were you?"

Wuseong looked at him shyly; his body was tense and guarded, as if ready to bolt.

"Were you worried?"

"Of course!" Gilho's voice shook. "You disappear with no note, no call . . . it's okay. You'll be okay."

Wuseong stood up, his arms still crossed. A goose feather stuck up from his hair.

Gilho's head thundered with confusion. He wanted the boy

to know that he was sorry, but he was too proud, too afraid to admit it.

Wuseong's eyes fastened on Taeyeong, absorbed by the Hugo Boss–clad, reclining misery, as if he were another species altogether. Wuseong smiled a bright, tired smile. "We should be going to bed."

Gilho patted the boy on the head. He almost patted the goose before he remembered that it was just a goose. He said something about his best bottle of Bordeaux. "I expect we'll drink to the morning."

Snow flurries fell against the glass. Gilho returned to the kitchen and clumsily chopped at a chunk of dried squid with a steak knife. Wuseong pressed his face against the glass. On the other side, Taeyeong rubbed his eyes and breathed heavily from the sofa. All of them, strangers in their lives, watched the wintering landscape.

A shriek shattered the silence. By the time Gilho bolted back to the living room, Taeyeong, his voice dancing with fear, was gripping his bleeding hand.

Wuseong hopped nervously from left leg to right.

"Your friend kept trying to pluck her," he said. "I tried to stop him, I did."

Taeyeong moaned. "One feather—I just wanted one. To see if you can really write with one of 'em."

Gilho headed straight for the balcony. Alcohol heightened his notion that a man should protect his friends; he was ready for a confrontation. As if it sensed his animosity, the goose trumpeted and hissed with its bill wide open; it charged, its wing billowing in the air like a stiff petticoat. Gilho grasped at the beating good wing, and felt the webbed feet on his foot. His hand seemed to reach through nothing, as if there were no body underneath the feathers. Its black pupils locked with his.

He gripped the goose's tubelike neck as best he could with both hands. It startled him to sense this immense power that one could have over life. In the haze of alcohol, he felt convinced that if this bulbous creature was extinguished with one twist, somehow his life would be simplified.

An unfamiliar shadow passed over Wuseong's face. It flickered, disappeared. He looked at Gilho as if he saw right through him, and forgave him for his cowardice.

Gilho released the goose and staggered back inside.

He said, "Why do you look at me like that?"

Taeyeong stared, his hand forgotten.

"Ajeoshi," Wuseong said wistfully, "the world's full of mystery— it's our duty to accept it."

Wuseong dashed to Taeyeong's side and inspected his hand. Gilho heard him humming as if he weren't completely alone in the world; as if he weren't living with an older man cracking up with love; as if a bleak future were not awaiting him. He hummed as if hope were enough to sustain him.

An hour into sleep Gilho woke up to the first full moon of the new year. He went to the kitchen for water, then standing with the empty glass he watched car beams flashing on the nearby riverside highway, alone with the lie that he was. He no longer wanted to be different from other men. As he turned to go he heard a muffled whisper from the living room. One figure, then two, moved on the balcony. There was a woman. She was around Gilho's age with hair as black as a coffin, a body thin and frail on top, with rotund legs. She rested her head against Wuseong's shoulder. Her face was weathered with dirt and death, but her eyes were generous and untroubled, her lips were a seamless line of perseverance. The cool moonlight brightened the balcony. As the boy's hand gathered around the woman's head, her face brightened. Gilho saw her attenuated fingers, her delicate, blue-tinted feet. He saw what he had been resisting all this time: the world through Wuseong's eyes.

Gilho took a step toward the balcony, then another. When he slid open the door, Wuseong looked up, unsurprised. He slipped his hand into Gilho's.

"Isn't my mother beautiful?" Wuseong said.

Gilho nodded, afraid to say anything. He breathed in shallow bursts.

"Ajeoshi, are you all right?"

Gilho rested his hand on the boy's shoulder.

He did not care that Taeyeong might stumble out of the guest room, looking for the bathroom. It was the first full moon of the new year, Daeboreum, the day hundreds of people hiked up the mountains to catch the rising of the moon for a year's worth of luck, and bonfire festivals replayed the fires of the past that had driven away evil spirits. Tonight the apartment was Gilho's mountain where he was caught in the moon's light. He was ready to go anywhere with Wuseong. Anywhere to be far from Gilho's position, the eyes of his parents, his friends, anywhere where they could be themselves. He wanted to ask the goose for forgiveness. For wanting her son in an unforgivable way. For being a married man betraying his family. Forgiveness, because he was prepared to scandalize. Tonight he was going to kiss the boy he loved. He turned to Wuseong.

"I've been lonely," he said, and shuddered, when the woman's arms, the goose's good, stiff feathers, circled over them. "I've been lonely all my life."

THE SALARYMAN

WHEN YOU ARRIVE at seven in the morning, your exhausted colleagues are already at their cubicles. Once again you stride past, trying to appear necessary. You are wearing the only suit you allowed your wife to buy at full price beyond your means, a navy wool blend with a red silk tie from Hyundai Department Store that disguises your stomach's pouch and your rural upbringing in Iksan of street markets and communal toilets.

On the way to your cubicle, you bow to Manager Han, who stares back with glazed eyes in what has become his only expression. He lost his savings in the plummeting company stocks, then lost his wife, and may be contemplating suicide. You, too, lost your savings, but thankfully didn't have much to lose. Ms. Min, the only woman in marketing with you, has divorced her husband, employed in the strategy planning department. You suspect this shameful state of her affairs is a paper divorce only, for companies like to fire married women who can rely on their husbands. Just last month, after his company released him, an acquaintance of yours drowned off Seongsu Bridge in the Han River. The truth of his suicide was muzzled so his wife and children could subsist on the life insurance money. Nightly the nine o'clock news parades such stories. These clips, rare to Korea before the 1997 IMF crisis destroyed the job-for-life policy, are suddenly so ordinary that when you attended your acquaintance's funeral, your mourning felt like a forgery.

As she does each morning Ms. Min delivers newspapers and memos across the floor. Perhaps because you have the kind of face that people easily forget, she smiles as if you two have just been introduced. This doesn't perturb you; being singled out is what flusters you. You turn the computer on, scan the memos, and admire your immaculate desk: documents arranged in color-coded files, books stacked on a two-tier shelf, pencils honed to fine points, all which accurately reflect the desk of a person who takes care in the work done. You have never pocketed a single office supply. Unlike your wife this morning, colleagues express pleasure in your company.

Your wife, Jayeong, began your day with kisses that traveled your neck before the children were awake and crawling into your double bed, but by breakfast she launched into you with talk of money. Children are expensive. Rent is expensive. She said if your parents had planned for their future, you wouldn't have to send a monthly allowance to them in Iksan. But they live off of what little money their alleyway eatery brings in and you are their only son, the one whom they worked hard to send to college, and they depend on you. You made the mistake of adding, well, what about her new scarf, the one designed by some Frenchman, that cost as much as your parents' monthly grocery bill? You suggested that she had unreasonable shopping habits.

Jayeong's eyebrows peaked. She said, "At least we don't have to support my family."

When necessary, she will remind you of this.

You wanted desperately to make her happy.

"I'm just a stingy *ajeoshi*," you said. "The scarf is perfect on you."

Yoona and Jeongmin interrupted to pin a parents' day pink chrysanthemum to your suit lapel. Jeongmin's feral eyes were milky with sleep as he balanced expertly on your feet. Yoona called out to him in a plummy voice, but the next moment, she pushed her brother aside and stood in his place. Even if she is a girl, she is your secret favorite, a scrappy beauty who once cried because she would never be able to personally meet Marie Curie.

They are five and seven and heavy, your burdens that you hoisted in your arms. You were smelling the garlic and ginger of their skin when Yoona said, "Appa, are you a drunkard?"

She has been listening too closely to the family's arguments.

The day is like any other day until Deputy Manager Kang calls you into his office.

When you open his door, Mr. Kang's squat fingers are spread out equidistant from one another. He is as pale as rice, and so short that his feet dangle from the ergonomic leather chair. More than once you have been tempted to push him off. When you apologize for your tardiness that day, he looks through you. He normally greets you with confidences, for you are capable, conscientious, and maintain a Swiss neutrality in the labyrinth of office politics. Though the company, like countless others, has declared bankruptcy and is restructuring, you had never imagined it would be you called to the office.

Still not looking at you, he says, "Assistant Manager Seo, once, our company was family for life. But with the IMF . . . now there are no guarantees."

You pick your ear with a ballpoint pen, as is your habit. You say, "I appreciate the warning."

"It's headquarters' orders." He squints over your shoulder. "You know I'm like an older brother to you, but your job . . . no longer exists."

Using his official work title, you say, "Bujang-nim, there must be an alternative."

"I'm sorry, Mr. Seo. It's a terrible time to live in."

He grips your hand and shakes it hard. He says something about trying to help you in any way he can, which embarrasses both of you. You bow mechanically. The entire time, his eyes lock on the clock, as if he no longer has time for a man whose future he has just erased.

You steal to Yeoido Park a few blocks from the office. On the benches men in suits are reading newspapers. You sit and, before you're asked, fabulate to the man next to you until the story of this prosperous company you own doesn't sound plausible even to you. It makes you angry, how each man in the park and in the libraries will come home to his family and say, Yeobo, work was fine, until there's no money left in the bank account. You feel the mandible crush in the endless lies they must tell, and swear not to be like them, though you, too, are thirty-five with two kids and a wife to support, little savings, a rental apartment, and now unemployed in the middle of an unprecedented financial crisis. Your company has abandoned you, but you are not finished.

At night you descend the bus and pass dozens of matchbox apartment blocks identical to yours, gaping commercial buildings, a playground. In the six years devoted to your company, you worked, ate, worked, ate. You drank because Mr. Kang, like most deputy managers, expects it; two reluctant drinks, a less reluctant third, then a fourth, and a fifth, on the corporate expense account. Late at night after you arrived home to the suburbs of Gunsan, near kilometers of apartments built so close to one another that you can see neighbors at night changing their clothes, you stopped at the playground and imagined yourself ten years later with the same company, returning to your wife and two college-age kids. You dreamed modestly.

In one hand you clutch a sable briefcase, and in the other, pink delphiniums. You make it as far as the stairs and stand there until the security guard asks, "Is something wrong, Mr. Seo?" You smile and wave at him.

In front of your door you listen for the sounds of your children. Yoona, the spirited, earnest one, is loudly arguing for Bach over Mozart. Your wife disagrees; she enjoys a good quarrel. And Jeongmin? He is too affable to care about right or wrong. As they debate, he may be rolling his rice into balls and feeding the complacent cat. You leave the flowers on the mat. You are a salaryman who works—worked—for a respectable company, so how can you confess that you can no longer support your family? You find a pay phone by the playground, and call home.

You've turned fragile in the last few hours; your wife's forceful greeting is enough to crack the porcelain veneer of calm you have maintained. Still, you tell her to take the substantial apartment deposit, the bankbook, and the children to her mother's house near the hills of Andong.

"Forget me," you say, but the underbrush of your voice thickens. You snap the cord against the phone box. "I'll be fine. I can come get you when prospects improve."

"Yeobo, don't be ridiculous. Come home," she says, her voice tender but querulous.

You allow that you specialize in the ridiculous: remember the bicycle ride you attempted drunk across the steep Kangwondo Mountains?

She hiccups, a sound you love.

But as she drills you on whether or not the company will release your pension, for new bankruptcy laws exempt it from its responsibilities, you imagine her anxiously tracking you as you skim newspaper ads. You remember the one year you were unemployed, and how the bitter potions of ground deer antlers and the heart of the rare Jirisan black bear (at least that's what the *hanuisa* told you as she mixed the medicinal herbs), the fortifying dog meat stews, and other *heem*-producing foods could not bring back the heat and light you normally shared with your wife. You can combat the long work hours, the company drinking, the children's demands for attention. You can bear anything but witness your incompetence, so you decide you would rather sleep in the park. You try to sound confident, but your voice breaks at the end of the conversation, and even to you, you seem pitiful.

————

At sunrise you queue behind hundreds of other men at an employment center. When you finally meet a public servant, he informs you that over two thousand people have applied for the advertised sanitation job. It's still a government job, he explains; the economy's paralyzed. The convenience stores and restaurants hire only young people for minimum wage. Other jobs require specialized knowledge such as interpretation skills or orthography. You do not have a fancy degree from overseas or parents who can support you. You do not speak three foreign languages. Still, you tell him that you are a college graduate, and have job experience. As a proud Daehan Minguk citizen you have mastered Korean and have competence in English. You fill out all available applications, though you are told not to be too hopeful.

Seoul Station may stink of urine and flesh and futility, the police may hound these subterranean arcade residents, the other city, but it keeps you warm, and this matters, for last night you woke up outside shivering with dew on your lashes. Now your back hugs the cold wall and drunk voices boom as you fish for your wallet with its family photos. But it has already been stolen. That's when you realize you are no longer needed.

You avoid conversation. When heading toward the bathroom, you arc away from the other men as if they are contagious. One man lies on his wasted face. Another must be at least sixty. Tiny indentations, like flecks of sea lice, discolor his neck and cheeks. A crust of mold growing between his toes smells of pickled radish; one black toenail is rotting off. He is old enough to be your father and in a sane society would have been cared for by his children. But Korea is no longer sane; you no longer feel sane.

The fluorescent arcade lights puncture your eyes; the subway bathroom line is unbearably long. You stand behind men who have lost their homes, or are fleeing the homes they have. Some hide tiny bars of soap and razors in their hands, and a few grip toothbrushes. Most laugh when you scrub your hair with paper towels. Over the months you will get used to standing in such long, senseless lines.

You get used to many things. For instance, queuing for a free meal at Tapgol Park before noon. Clearing out of the chilly arcade each morning when the police hustle you. Estimating time by studying the sun after your watch battery gives up. Trudging to the job center. Digging in the scree of the city dump for edibles and clothing. Finding an occasional bed in a shelter. Begging. When you have money, drinking the alcohol that during your regimented corporate years has become necessary to you. Waking up underground to the bitter bouquet of your comrades' bodies in monsoon season. For you have found a few comrades by now.

It is sometime in late July or August. When you wake up, Yeongsuk offers you and Daehoon *soju*. The cheap rice wine burns and you sip only enough to take the edge off of waking slick in your own sweat. Yeongsuk has pale, aristocratic skin, a portly, graceful carriage, and lynx's eyes disguised behind thick glasses. He won't return home out of shame, for just before the crisis, he had taken the bulk of his parents' retirement fund and traded and lost his savings, as well as theirs, in futures. He is alarmingly generous with his food and alcohol, a habit you have found rare in those who come from plentitude. Even now he urges you to accept half a stick of gum.

Daehoon takes a long swig from the bottle, then flexes his considerable biceps before beginning his exercises. He is a twenty-seven-year-old nonunionized worker who punched you in the nose the one time you asked about his family. In between sets of push-ups and a half dozen different exotic sit-ups, he struts around in bleached jeans that hug his testicles. His barrel chest protrudes over a girl-size waist; he often scratches himself generously while you're looking. When you've had a few drinks, you allow that he is "entertaining," and though you would rather not wake up each morning to his trucker's mouth, you do feel safer with him. In their company, you do not feel as lonely.

After Daehoon completes a third set of fifty push-ups, he bounds up and spits a wad of thick jelly, which vaults onto your shoe. You are secretly pleased that you cut off too much from his hair yesterday, which now tufts up at the top.

He says, "They say if you get yourself in debt to a gang and can't pay, they chop off your legs and make you beg for a living. Pick you up, drop you off, give you food and a bed. Not a bad life."

"Without legs?" you say. "You can't do push-ups with no legs."

You fear those men, some of them debtors and industrial accident casualties, and still others neglected Vietnam veterans from back in the seventies who, with their stumps wrapped in thick industrial rubber, propel their torsos by skateboard. You dread their clawing hands, their truculent faces. In dreams, they suffocate you with their gutted legs.

Daehoon slaps his heavy thighs. "These two stumps, are they doing anything for me right now?"

"I'd rather go to America and do hard work," says Yeongsuk. "Perhaps drive trucks or labor on a chicken farm. Perhaps even get another finance job."

"America!" Daehoon snorts. "And I'm President Roh Tae-woo! You got the kind of money to pay off visa sharks?"

"And what if I do?"

"I don't care about your fancy foreign suit covered in dirt, or your fancy education," says Daehoon. "If they let you in, I'm capable of marrying me a rich bitch from the Kangnam neighborhood. I'd just as soon chop off my legs, sell what I've got."

"Did you know that on the black market, one of your kidneys could be valued at over twenty thousand dollars?" says Yeongsuk. "That's at least thirty million won. No, near forty, I think, with the present currency devaluation."

Both of you stare at him. Yeongsuk entertains himself by doing things like reciting the periodic table, tracing word etymologies, and deducing the possible whereabouts of former dictator Chun Du-hwan's reputed illegal fortune of two hundred million U.S. dollars. He knows the strangest things.

At noon the three of you head toward Jongro where a thin meat-bone soup and rice will be served by humorless Christians. Past enormous yellow cranes that slumber over the many halted building projects, already the line weaves around the block. That doesn't stop Daehoon from cutting in front of the smallest, youngest man he finds.

The man, though slight and stringy, collars Daehoon and says, *"Gaesaekki!"*

He stitches curses together so quickly it sounds like a foreign language. The man drives back Daehoon, who clearly expected instant capitulation.

The man adds in *ban-mal,* his language casual and disrespectful, "It's *saekkis* like you I hate."

"Who're you using *ban-mal* to?" Daehoon cocks his fists. "You're talking to someone older than you!"

You secretly wish that Daehoon will be vanquished; it is difficult to like a man who mimics your high-pitched voice when you are excited and tells you that you walk like a woman. He is so large, he makes you feel insufficient. But there are too many people watching and he cannot lose face, so he grabs the man's shirt and caroms into him. Only after Yeongsuk pokes you with a chopstick, you help drag Daehoon off to the side. He struggles just enough to show he is eager to fight.

The pickled radish is fresh and spicy, the clear, meaty broth salty and smooth, but Yeongsuk, as usual, eats rapidly, then rises. He will call his parents and his wife, as he does every week, pretending to be in America. He will tell his parents that he, the oldest son, is their guarantee. He will promise to bring his wife over after he gets settled. When you once asked how he can lie so creatively, he said that he's not, quite, for he has set aside an emergency fund and paid a reputable immigration company. Give me time, he said equably. Even though he went to graduate school and was an investment banker and knows many useless things, you don't believe him.

After the soup is gone, you think about Jayeong, the children. You touch your inner suit pocket where the dried chrysanthemum rests. You miss your wife's rapturous laughter, sleeping against her soft, irregular snores that wake you up. You even miss the arguments.

Daehoon watches the fan above and demonstrates his usual conversational skills by wondering if your skull would split apart if it fell off. When you tell him that you will return in five minutes, he grins as he scrapes Yeongsuk's and your leftovers into his bowl. He is as hefty as a wedding chest; maybe that is why his constant hunger disgusts you. You straighten your yellowed collar and sling the briefcase over your shoulder. From a distance you are still a salaryman.

"Hello? Who's speaking?"

It is Jayeong. Since you hang up if your mother-in-law picks up, it has been a month since you two have spoken. Her small, quick hands, her arms of pressed lavender and lavish, dogmatic certainty; you can almost smell them.

You deposit your last coins. "Yeobo, it's me."

"Yeobo? Are you safe?" Her voice strains with forced welcome, and you hear this immediately.

"What's wrong?"

There is a silence.

You say would it hurt to be a little positive? She has the warm bed, and she has the children. You force a laugh. She responds that she has been thinking. She recounts your drinking and the cycle of debt. The money you sent your in-laws. The creditors that have begun circling. Now this. The debt, you say, helped pay for the children that she'd wanted. You are startled by your cowardice, your cruelty.

She says, "They say more than half of divorces are about money."

The word *divorce* silences you for a moment. "Who are 'they'?" you finally say.

"I need to protect myself and our babies. They'll take the money that's left if it's in your name. If I'm not careful . . . Others are doing the same, too. It's just a piece of paper."

Your armpits become hot. You start to see white spots. Odd, you say, how a man loses value overnight without a salary.

She says, "It's not about that, not at all. I can't be derailed this time."

You say, even over the phone, you can smell her lavender and garlic.

She says something about Seoul and court documents and how she needs a guarantee against any possible future debt of yours; you retort that she is being capricious as usual. You say that she will regret this tomorrow, so let's just not continue. She persists, so you begin chanting some of Yeongsuk's etymologies of words over her rising cant. You cannot let her continue because your family is your last possibility for a world that seems more and more distant. You cannot listen because losing your wife will rend the little left of you. You will not because you want to live.

When she says, "Please, please cooperate, don't make me crazier than I already feel," you hang up.

The passing crowds overwhelm you—their talk of school and meetings and weekend plans. All these ordinary people with their lives intact.

You enter the nearest convenience store and open up a bottle of *soju* and drink it right there between the Pringles and the dried cuttlefish. After you pay the clerk with your last bills, you spit on a hairdresser's towels hanging outside on a clothes rack. The world you see is your enemy. You kick the glass doors of each business establishment, determined to break one in. You only bruise your toe.

In the morning you still visit the employment center because that, at least, is reliable. Miraculously, they are able to set up an interview for you. They require someone with computer skills and job experience, no advanced degree. That is you exactly. But you are a little nervous. Last night you almost called your wife, but instead you drank with your comrades.

Yeongsuk coaches you once again on interview techniques and tucks bus fare and a little lucky money into your inner jacket pocket. You call him Older Brother for the first time, and mean it.

After you arrive at the interview, you wait with hundreds of other applicants. Your suit is freshly pressed and your hair washed and cut, but you slur when you speak. You hadn't meant to but you were so nervous. When you had stopped by the store on the way to the interview, you had meant to have only one little sip.

By fall, you agree to meet your wife. You washed as best you could, shaved, shined your shoes and briefcase, and while strolling through the department store sprayed yourself with a sample of Ralph Lauren Polo cologne. You almost look presentable. You had come to the designated café in a gentler neighborhood of Seoul braced to finesse, to persuade, to argue if necessary. But you lose confidence as soon as Jayeong arrives. Those are wild, uncertain eyes, desperate for change. She has even armed herself with the children, dressed in their Sunday finery, which you had not prepared for.

Yoona hangs back shyly, but on command pecks your cheek. Afterward, she darts back as if afraid of you. "Appa," she says, "your eyes are red and you smell funny."

You clutch her palm but still feel stained with the stench of the streets. As you present Yoona with pink delphiniums, you say, "That's because Appa's been up all night picking these for you."

"When things are better for you, you can give Yoona flowers anytime." Your wife's voice is brisk and vigilant. "We're ready to come back anytime, really anytime you want."

"Visit?" Yoona pulls at her lace collar as if to tear it. "No more visits! Let's all go home!"

But you know that there is no home to return to, and Jayeong is right to have made up her mind. There are the remaining assets and the children to protect. When your wife rises, it seems impossible that you once knew her body so well.

Along with the divorce papers, she presses an envelope into your hands—money, as you knew it would be—and though you will regret it later, you throw her charity at her. It slaps her chest and falls, scattering King Sejong's somber face across the floor like nightclub advertisements.

Her arms tremble; as she picks up the money, you flounder in your dark thoughts. The children have gone so still and quiet, they do not seem like children.

You tug at the top button on your jacket until it comes off in your hand.

"You need it more than we do," she says.

"Don't make me pathetic!"

Your agitated hands knock down the house of sugar cubes that Jeongmin has built, which makes him cry. You are astonished and ashamed by your ability to hurt them. Your wife hugs Jeongmin with her right arm and Yoona with her left, calming them.

"Keep your mind together," she says. "Think of the children."

You are, you are thinking of yourself without them. You touch your children's faces, then yours, making sure that all of you are still there. You want to hold Yoona, but that will break you. So you kiss Jeongmin's cheeks. You restack the sugar cubes.

You tell Yoona, "This is what our house will look like when we live together."

Though Yoona's hands ball up on her hips, her mouth prim with suspicion, Jeongmin, for whom the past is already forgotten, struggles into your lap.

He says, "Appa, I can read now."

He can read, and you were not there to teach him.

It is winter when you skid across an ice patch. Yeongsuk is gone. He secured a visa to America after all. In your drowsy, drunkenness you miss him. You no longer visit the employment center. You have forgotten why you wanted a job in the first place. Late at night, you raid the bags of those new to Seoul Station while they sleep. You take money, *soju,* napkins, anything of use, just as people once stole from you. Outside, when winds scissor through your clothes, you warm up beside vendors firing chestnuts and sweet potatoes over coals, and when you walk the Han River's many bridges, you occasionally entertain jumping.

When you are sober you think about your parents, or Jayeong. You now think that your wife, now ex-wife, since you finally went to city hall and signed the documents, was right to leave you. You, a docile fool, had believed that if you worked hard enough, you could protect those you loved.

The drinking makes you content. The pavement is warm even when the Siberian winds hook into your skin; the universe and its people love you when you drink. You will do anything for a drink. Sometimes you prowl large discount stores and filch *soju* from the stacked aisles. If someone sees you, you go to jail for a few days where they feed you regularly. You even like Daehoon when you're drunk.

But when you are not drunk, you wish you were brave enough to be alone. Just yesterday Daehoon told you with his usual cheeriness, "People care more about their hairstyles than a dead stranger." During slow hours he demonstrates his one-handed push-up and tells you with a bravado you despise that you're lucky because if he wanted to, he could really hurt you.

In Gwanghwamun most people, still unused to the sudden swell in the number of homeless, are embarrassed by you. You had first constructed a cardboard sign that read: WILL WORK FOR FOOD. You had crouched in front of the sign to hide your face, your hands outstretched to these people with jobs and families who marched up the stairs, who did not look left or right. Someone stepped over your legs. Now you wear a sign that says: I AM DEAF AND DUMB. PLEASE HELP ME. You walk up to people, hand outstretched, and shame them into giving.

It is rush hour, the time of day when you stare boldly at women in their dry-cleaned dresses and suck in their scented soap and hold the smells. A year has passed since you have been in the company of women.

Among all these untouchable women, you spot Haemin Lee,

who studied marketing with you at university. She sports no wedding band. Like many women, in a surge of patriotism she has probably donated her jewelry to the government in order to reduce the national deficit. It is a shock, remembering what you have lost, especially when she recognizes you and her face is transformed by pity, a look that follows you everywhere. You hide behind the waves of your shoulder-length hair.

"Obba!"

She calls you Older Brother as she used to, and noses her way down until her almond-shaped face is level with yours. Her once lovely features now submit to gravity.

"Dear Lord." Her breath warms your ear. "How could this happen to you?"

With your face averted and your cap out, in your best imitation of a Busan accent, you say, "Please, help me. I've spilled my soup, all of it."

"Obba." She steps back. Already, there is curiosity to her pity. "Is it you?"

You realize that you, too, are no longer the man that Haemin knew, not the student who once saved up for summer cycling trips, not the student who feebly demonstrated against the military regime in order to skip a day of classes. You no longer play folk music or believe in progress. You became a salaryman. And now you are not even that.

Something drops into your hat. The sound, a soft rustle, is bills.

You keep your eyes to the ground but touch her skirt. "Haemin," you say. "Thank you."

"It's all I have right now," she says, apologetic for being a witness. The next train of commuters, rising up from underground like riot police, pushes her along.

Your cap now cradles five mint-green bills. Fifty thousand won total. Enough for twenty bottles of *soju* and at least a dozen cups of instant ramen. Or? They say money can even buy testicles on a female virgin. You rub the bills against your papery cheeks. With this money you have choices.

Daehoon, crouched on cobbled newspapers opposite, stares at you. His sign says: INDUSTRIAL LAYOFFS. AM FEEDING A FAMILY OF THREE.

"Listen," he says. "Where you're sitting—that was my spot. It's been my spot almost every day."

You bury the money in your briefcase. "You have a land deed?"

He stands up, agitated. He says, "At least share."

" 'Sharing,' " you quote him, " 'is for losers who can't protect what they've got.' "

For the rest of the day Daehoon refuses to speak to you. You are used to this. For a twenty-seven-year-old, he is quite childish.

It may be two or three in the morning when you wake to a rustling. You think it is a mouse until you see Daehoon rifling through your briefcase that you had fallen asleep hugging. With his bag and your briefcase over his shoulder, he is preparing to flee. You will not let him do this to you. The green bills separate you from who you were the day before, and you want to live because you are a human being and you deserve it.

He pivots away as you sit up, but you manage to hold on to the bag's strap. You claw at your bag with both hands and butt him with your head. He only steps back a few inches, ready now with a pocketknife, the blade flipped up. With a wild kick, you knock it skittering out of his hand and across the cement. You trip him and land on top of his chest, your right hand roped around his throat, and take his fast, furious blows while your left hand gropes in your bag for anything that you can trust. "Help!" you shout, but everyone near you is asleep, or pretending to be. He pries you off and grips you one-handed by the throat and holds you up like a hanged man. As you gag, saliva pooling at the corners of your mouth, he laughs and says, "You're dead, princess," as he lowers you to the floor. That's when you touch the metal chopsticks in your briefcase and thrust them into his stomach with both hands as far as you can. He doubles over, looking astonished and a little ashamed that he has permitted this. You feel a small pleasure in stopping his laughter.

The chopsticks jut out from his belly. A triangle of blood blooms beneath your shoes. You touch your right hand flecked with blood and bow down to his heaving body. You did not know chopsticks could enter so deeply.

The chopsticks are valuable to you so you hold him by the shoulder, pull them out, and wipe the coat of blood against his shirt. He grunts twice, eyes wide open. As you look for money in his bag, take the pocketknife, rummage for anything that might be useful, he calls your name. You cannot look at him. You run, you flee, gripping your briefcase of belongings and your precious blanket.

You are a human being, a human being, human. Being.

DRIFTING HOUSE

T HE DAY THE siblings left to find their mother, snow devoured the northern mining town. Houses loomed like ghosts. The government's face was everywhere: on the sides of a marooned cart, above the lintel of the gray post office, on placards scattered throughout the surrounding mountains praising the Dear Leader Kim Jong-il. And in the grain sack strapped to the oldest brother Woncheol's back, their crippled sister, the weight of a few books.

The younger brother, Choecheol, ran ahead. Like a child, Woncheol thought, frowning, though he was also a child, an eleven-year-old with a body withering on two years of boiled tree bark, mashed roots, and the occasional grilled rat and fried crickets on a stick. He picked across the public square, afraid to step where last month the town had watched two men dragged in, necklaces of bones, and hanged for cannibalizing their parents. They passed a vendor and woman haggling as if on the frontier of madness. On the straw mat between them, one frozen flank of beef? Pork? Or human? No one knew anymore, though they pretended to.

"She's slowing us down," Choecheol whined as he circled back. "We'll be dead before we reach China."

Woncheol tied his brother's laces in symmetrical bows. "Shut up," he said. For younger children obeyed the older one who obeyed the mother who obeyed the father who obeyed the Dear Leader. For the school textbooks stated that a swallow had descended from heaven at the Dear Leader's birth, that trees bloomed and snow melted in the Dear Leader's presence. He stubbornly ignored the salmon fishery and the town's vegetable gardens that the soldiers guarded, shooting intruders on sight. For there was an order to everything. Or there used to be.

Still, he soldiered his siblings up the mountain slope of granite and bare, spectral trees with the assurance of an oldest son. His legs shook under his sister's slight weight. As they continued, the town's narrow harmonica houses, the empty factories, even the glorious statue of Kim Il-sung, their Great Leader and the Dear Leader's father, shrank to the size of a thumbnail. Then their town was gone. He labored with his back heavy with Gukhwa's weight, his face scraped raw with exposure to the weather, until his knees buckled once, twice, in the snow. Ahead of them were only the white backs of the mountain range, and the Tumen River still nowhere in sight. He could carry her no farther.

Choecheol walked ahead, his nose so close to the ground as he looked for acorns, he passed one near his shoe. Woncheol picked it up and waited until his brother was deep in the forest before he set his sister on a hillock of granite. While he struck the nut against a rock, she watched with the expectancy of someone who knew she was loved. The Tumen River to China would be frozen for crossing, and he had to make the necessary sacrifices. He knew this, but still he peeled the woody skin back a thin strip at a time. The acorn's meat wrinkled and gray. The size of a rat's brain. He broke it into nearly perfect thirds, and into her waiting, open mouth, fed Gukhwa the largest chunk. His hands were shaking. It was good, without insects.

"Obba, where are birds?" Gukhwa said, her breath a sick hiss.

"You *babo,* it's too cold for birds." He was angry because she still trusted him.

Then he remembered her thirst and scooped up some snow, which she licked off his palm.

"Obba, it hurts." She stuck her frozen yellowed tongue out for inspection. "Obba," she said again, and smiled, a little, as if the words *older brother* were a song she liked to sing.

He cleaned her face with his mittens, softly scraped under her fingernails with pine needles. Reminded himself again how impossible it would be to carry her on the long walk to China. Then he closed his eyes, twisted their mother's scarf around Gukhwa's neck, and choked her. It was better this way, he was convinced, than to leave her afraid, starving slowly to death. He did not let go until she stopped moving.

Oldest Son, please forgive my selfishness, his mother had written. *You're their mother and father now.* No one but them, in the village created after the Korean War for those the government called the wavering or hostile class, was surprised when their mother fled a week ago. She, a woman rumored to pollute her widowed flesh by selling herself to feed her three children, was only following the thousands escaping to China after the government stopped food rations altogether in 1997. Hunger changed people, destroyed the strongest bonds between parents and children, and young and old, and a woman with disgraced flesh was already a broken woman. As the old saying went, *If you starve three days, there is no thought that does not invade your imagination*. But Woncheol believed they would find her, the way he believed in the sky and the snow, the American imperialists that the Dear Leader said were starving the country out of existence. It was so inconceivable to be without his mother, he had even sacrificed his sister.

But with the sack now the weight of a house, a squid boat, Woncheol could not give up as planned. He lugged the sack with her body across rock and ridge, his hands burning through his mittens, until he couldn't any longer. In the sun his cheekbones were nearly visible through the stretched skin. Gukhwa's fingers were still haunting his back.

"What do we do?" he said. "What did I do wrong?"

Choecheol's face was blank with waiting because his *hyeong*, his older brother, always knew what to do.

But Woncheol only stared at the sack.

"We can't bury her," he finally said. "The ground's all rock."

The downbeat of his words skittered across the icy plain. Choecheol pivoted away. Eyes wild for escape.

He sang, "One dead American plus one dead American equals two dead Americans," while crushing snow into powder, trying to distract Woncheol.

But it was time. Woncheol turned back the lip of the sack. She tumbled out. He moved his hands over Gukhwa's face, unable to comprehend what he had done. He could only look at her a fragment at a time. Her cheeks the shade of boiled snails. Her arms two stiff twigs.

"I can do my arithmetic," Choecheol sang. "One dead American—"

Woncheol forced his brother's face close. Their sister's forehead was stippled with sores. She was so quiet, and each moment that passed there seemed to be a little less of her than before.

"Look hard," he said. "She's gone."

His brother stopped. His eyes as blank as coffin lids.

"Ten comrades died this year," Choecheol said. He smiled so hard he became teary from the effort. "If I don't think about her, she's not there."

Their baby sister. The sun, dancing on Woncheol's chilled face, changed Gukhwa into polished bone. Into something unworldly, numinous. Once he had fed and bathed her, had been her drifting house. Something stirred in him, a memory of an earlier time. The trees, heavy with swallows. When the birds rose into the air, the trees lifting with them. His sister's feet the size of a swallow. Swallows, they could go anywhere, his mother had said, but they returned because it was their home. Suddenly Woncheol was afraid.

"I killed her." He said this with surprise.

"You—didn't—kill—anyone!" Choecheol covered his ears and began to sing.

Woncheol began folding the sack in neat creases. The praise of his teachers, his mother's trust. Nothing could help him now. He folded until Choecheol complained of the cold, his blue-tinted lips puckered like an old *halmeoni* looking for her teeth.

Only then Woncheol took two fistfuls of snow. He smoothed

it down over his sister and all his memories. He added fistful after fistful until he could no longer feel the cold. Added snow until a shape grew resembling the tumulus graves of their ancestors. He stepped back and circled the mound, watching it.

Sooner or later, everyone in town heard the stories about those who crossed the border and returned with a miracle of money and food. There were stories of an ironmonger Lee safe in something called an embassy, or rice-cake-turned-grass-cake-vendor Miss Han furtively married to a Chinese farmer, despite the Chinese government's bounty on North Korean heads. But Mrs. Ku with child was beaten off the U.S. embassy gates by the Chinese police. Woojin, a boy of eight, was killed by border guards. Someone called Daejon's uncle, drowned in the monsoon-swollen Tumen River to China. A young and beautiful Seoyeon (they were always young and beautiful in the whispered stories), raped but lucky to be alive. Thirteen-year-old Sora, caught and sold by Chinese traffickers. Which meant rape, too, Seungwoo's aunt had said. Whether any of this was actually true, no one knew, the same way they silently speculated whether someone was an ally or informer, or whether someone who disappeared in the night had been imprisoned or sent to a reeducation camp or had escaped to China, and watched and waited as the rumors turned into hardened truth.

Still, as the sun set, the two black dots moved across the great white back of the mountain's summit, past the last stately granite boulders carved with the Great Leader Kim Il-sung's and the Dear Leader Kim Jong-il's epithets. The brothers unknowingly moved in the same path that their mother had embarked on a month ago when she had made her terrible decision, followed the ghostly steps of others whose hunger had strained their allegiances to family, to country, to love. Behind Woncheol his brother struggled from rock to rock. So small, Woncheol thought, so breakable, turning every few minutes to watch his brother's progress as if he would lose him if he stopped looking.

"Careful!" he said, afraid for him.

"Yes, Hyeong."

After a few hours they rested.

"I'm wet all over," Choecheol complained, as he kept trying to strip, but Woncheol made sure his brother kept his hands mittened in socks.

It happened when Woncheol looked for walking sticks. As he wandered between the trees, a white apparition lumbered into him. Its sound an unearthly menace. Fear hooked his throat like a fish bone and he screamed, his hands helmeted his head. But it was Choecheol, laughing. His hair, shoulders, banked with crystals of snow, gave him a phantom look.

"Babo," Woncheol said, almost weeping from fear.

She was only four, she was his sister. He had loved her. He dumped an armful of snow on his brother's head. He said, "You stink of American feet."

"I scared you." Choecheol's voice peaked nervously. "There's nothing to scare us, is there?"

As they walked, the rocks took on shapes. "Over there," Woncheol said. "See the pigs?"

He pointed at the gray-pink ears pinned back as the fatty snouts rooted for food.

"You mean that patchy one, that speckly runt?" Choecheol pointed at a rock canopied in snow. "Kill it! Eat it!"

They giggled now, unable to stop.

"And when he walks, his balls wiggle," Woncheol said. "They're melons!"

His brother pantomimed a melon-balled, strutting pig.

Woncheol laughed, hot with happiness, until his thoughts migrated to his sister. He stopped laughing.

They continued west. The wind bellowed. The pine needles were tiny fingers. The crunch of snow, powdery bones. Even with newspaper crushed into his ears, he heard the whispering of *Obba. Obba.* From all four sides she seemed to call him.

Other visions followed.

The bushes keened with animal sounds. He whirled, a rubber band out of his pocket ready to fire. But there was no squirrel, no soldier casting a fatal shadow; it was only their sister. Her pallid skin. She leaped from rock to rock like a fawn. She smiled and wiggled her tiny fingers at him in the air, showing him, no hands! His breath came in ragged gasps. Still, her waifish form stood before him. He could not stop staring at the gourd shape of her forehead, her face of ivory varnish. She pulled a thread, unraveled her entire sweater before his next breath. Naked, her body flamed blue with heat. She bent until the back of her head brushed her heel, made an exaggerated shiver. The same Gukhwa, comic even in her revenge.

"The most revered mountain in Joseon," Woncheol muttered. "Baekdu Mountain, where our Great Leader Kim Il-sung was born. The second most worthy flower, Kimjongilia."

The school routines, the lists of facts that he had recited faster than anyone in his class, helped normalize his breathing.

But she was still there.

"I'm a Joseon soldier," he said louder now. "I'm a revolutionary warrior."

It was wrong, so wrong. Still, he propped his elbow on his shaking knee.

He squinted, rubber band aimed.

His brother followed him the way he often did. He made his hands into a machine gun, targeted a denuded fir tree. "I'm getting myself a Big Nose," he said, and popped off each potential American.

Woncheol aimed the rubber band, shot. She darted behind a tree; he hurtled behind a knot of rocks.

"Are you scared?" Choecheol looked ashamed for him. His legs spread out at an exaggerated distance as if to show that he would not go hiding behind rocks. Then he clambered through her.

"Watch out!" Woncheol cried.

"Watch what? The soldiers catch us, they kill us." Choecheol struck his foot outward in a crescent kick. "That's all."

"It's Gukhwa," Woncheol said.

His brother stiffened, stepped back. "There're no ghosts here," he said loudly.

Woncheol shot out again; it went straight through her. Gukhwa's laugh was a baby's gurgle that stopped abruptly. He covered his face with his hands, seeing the lumpy grain sack.

"We have to go back," Woncheol said. "We were crazy to try."

"Do you want to die?" said Choecheol. His voice was newly sharp. He stepped on his brother's shadow. "I want to live."

Woncheol looked west to China, a country where somewhere, he had a mother. There were a great many things he didn't know, he realized, and as he gazed at the horizon of splintered peaks, his life shrank in significance. He squeezed his hands behind his back until they stopped trembling.

"Then let's go," he said, forceful enough to reassure his brother.

Choecheol reemerged, brambles in his hair. He stood at unsteady attention. A drunk cadet.

"Yes, comrade!" he cried. His voice ballooned with relief.

The night was a black glove. The mountains an endless rubble of loose stones. The stars the eyes of the dead. In the unnatural landscape the one day felt as long as Woncheol's entire life. None of this mattered when Gukhwa began chanting his name.

He covered his ears. His mind was wild with cannonball thoughts.

Gukhwa's face was swollen like a pincushion, her ashen toes braced against tree roots like a seagull perching on a rock.

"I want to sleep." Choecheol sat beside Gukhwa in the snow, his legs out like chopsticks. "I'll do anything to sleep."

"If we sleep, we die." Woncheol stared at his two siblings, his loving burdens.

"I want to sleep."

"Just a few hours . . ."

"Sleep." His voice was high-pitched.

"You won't listen to your *hyeong*?" He was reduced to pleading.

"But I can't move." His brother flopped into a drift of snow to prove it.

"A few minutes, then. Then we go."

Once children had obeyed the mother who obeyed the father who obeyed the Dear Leader. But the systems had fallen apart.

Woncheol drew a box in the whiteness around them. They huddled on the patch of dryness.

"We aren't far," he said, though he did not know where they were. He spoke with the false calm of an older brother.

"I wish we had a big rat," said Choecheol. He looked up hopefully at Woncheol. "We could roast it on the fire."

"Me, too."

Woncheol tilted his head, filled his mouth with snow. The sting woke up his sleeping tongue, made it throb.

"It tastes like cold rice," he said, though he did not remember the taste of rice.

"If we had an ear of corn . . . two! Roasted."

"Don't let's talk about food."

His brother picked his nose, considered the wet curl of mucus before twirling it into his mouth. He said, "Do Chinese people really eat children's brains?"

"They don't need to," he said. "They are a land of rice bowls the size of you. That's what people say."

He said this, though he did not know who these people were; he had only his mother's word and the stories that grew out of the mouths of other kids hustling in the market; a hope kindled, flickering dead, then rekindled by a snatch of a word, or by the brief appearance of smuggled grain sold in the new, illegal markets.

"They eat rice every day there. That's what the older boys said."

"You saw what Omma brought back the first time."

"Where is she?" Choecheol hugged himself.

"Nobody knows." Woncheol wrapped his arms around his brother and gazed west toward where China must be. "Get some rest."

They slept. Woncheol's dreams had gone with his memories. There was no mother to haunt him with two large sacks of rice in her hands, releasing the grains that fell like snow. There was no father who made birdcalls that brought the village swallows settling onto his arms. There was only the emptiness of sleep, a peaceful forever, as if his body desired to become part of the snowy landscape and, over time, become the soil for another generation. But a sharp movement like teeth sinking into his arm ended the quiet.

He rolled Choecheol deep into a snowdrift. Then he jumped on the darkness, his boot smashed at where the nose must be. Underneath him, his walking stick. His arms swung up, down. A pestle to corn. He struck and struck. He could have stopped, but didn't.

"I'm a revolutionary warrior!" Choecheol's voice buckled. "I'm a Joseon soldier!"

Only then Woncheol stopped, looked at his brother's head just above the snowdrift. A thread of mucus hung from Choecheol's nose. He was crying. His own brother, afraid of him. And below Woncheol's feet, there was nothing. Only the withered trees and his shadow, gaunt and trembling in the moon's light. He stuffed snow in his mouth when a scream escaped him. Choecheol clumsily put his arms around him, but he pulled away.

"We'll never find her," Woncheol said. "Omma left us. The way we left Gukhwa."

"Hyeong, don't say that!"

But Woncheol was crying because he knew it was true.

Choecheol kicked a stone downhill. It rolled until their sister stopped it with her feet. Powdered in snow, she looked like a small, icy spirit. A chill smothered Woncheol.

"There's Gukhwa again," he said.

"She's a dead body." Choecheol shored himself up. "She's someone who's gone far away."

"She's right there!"

"There's no such thing as ghosts!" His brother charged ahead. "She's dead, she's dead, she's dead!"

"Wait for me!" Woncheol cried. Afraid alone, he followed him.

The next morning, the Tumen River. There was the hike down, the dangerous rustle of leaves. Guards were in outposts or on patrol, armed with Kalashnikovs and canvas boots. From an escarpment above, Woncheol watched. Beyond the endless mountains was Yanji, a city where it was said that the garbage could feed entire villages and the streetlights actually worked. There was also Gukhwa, as cold as stone. Their father, embalmed beneath the roof of coal that had collapsed on him. The world, forever dark for them both. And Woncheol was still alive; he did not know why he deserved it.

Noon. The brothers began the descent toward the river. Snow fell steadily, erasing their traces. The phalanx of guards had their cozy outposts, their rice. Woncheol assumed that their uniforms would dry over lunch; they would want to stay indoors and not get wet. Still, his heart was too fast. He muffled the sound with his hands. They passed a glassy waterfall. Their fingernails chipped, their hands bled from the rocks. They moved from roots of spruce and fir. Slowly. The iciness in his feet traveled through his body.

Finally. Before them was a gray landscape. They were meager shapes before they became a river, mountains, China. In the distance was a desolation of cement buildings so tall and crowded together, a person could disappear, never be found. The brothers stood where so many had stood in the past five years, and felt the same fugitive fears and hopes, the same dim sense that the world outstretched before them would never know or care about them.

"You were a good *hyeong*," Choecheol said, his voice heavy.

"I'll never make you eat arrowroot porridge again," Woncheol said. "We'll live differently."

He did not know how to speak this muddy love and fear he had for his brother, so he held his hand tightly, then let go.

They ran. They pitched into the clearing. Dashed toward the river. When their feet touched the ice beneath the snow, they skidded and fell.

"Halt!" a voice shouted. "*Meomcheo,* or I'll shoot!"

The man was small from a distance; he looked like a toy soldier in his uniform and starred cap, a rifle slung over his shoulder like a schoolbag. He hefted the gun up. Stop, stop, Woncheol's glottis throbbed. The man aimed ahead at Choecheol, zigzagging across the ice, and pulled the trigger.

There was the sharp shriek of a bullet, then nothing. No one had been hit.

Woncheol choked.

"Run!" he shouted as he slid across the plate of ice.

Choecheol looked back at him, now frozen.

"Hyeong," he said. He was crying.

"Your *hyeong* said run!"

And Choecheol ran, his light feet delicate on the ice. Each time he looked back, Woncheol shouted as he skidded, until finally his little brother was too far ahead to see.

Woncheol continued to skid forward, heavier and slower than Choecheol. His sister bounded in front of him. Her candle-wax eyes, bright and white as the core of a fire. Her cheeks now flamed—the only color in her stony face.

"Please let me go," he begged.

She reached into her small gray mouth, drew out a maggot, and flung it at him.

Her tiny legs stayed squarely planted between him and China. He moved left; so did she. He moved right; she mirrored him. When he stepped back, she relaxed into a smile. She did not want him to leave her to become one of the forgotten ones. He saw this now. His hand rose to strike her away, and her face rushed to a sad place. He could not do it. She was his sister; he would never forget her, so he extended his hands toward her ruined body.

Across the frozen river, the thud of an approaching soldier's steps faded as Woncheol now saw the phantom world that had always been there. His schoolteacher scraped bark from the air. His best friend, Gunhyeok, flush with his good luck, skinned and roasted a squirrel. While the sun was eclipsed by his father's swallows, their family home drifted across the ice. The chimney smoke smelled of his mother's vinegary cabbage, her loamy earth scent. There was his father wearing his salty smile, strolling beside countless, diaphanous figures. And behind them, there were the shadows.

A SMALL SORROW

1988. WHILE PEOPLE became used to the country's new, com-promised democracy, and their disappointed conversations revolved around the transfer from a dictator to the dictator's friend, Eunkang shrank into her compromised marriage. She was tired of smelling strange women on her husband and feeling like a desperate forty-year-old housewife, and not the professional art-ist that she was. So when her in-laws surprised them with a tradi-tional house skirting the DMZ belt that divided Korea, for once Eunkang had not resisted their extravagance. Her marriage, she had believed, would finally be safe away from Seoul. She was wrong. Only a month after their move, she watched her husband, Seongwon, in their spacious *hanok*'s main *sarang* courtyard, his arms around a girl dressed like a shiny birthday present.

The girl was as long as a grain of brown rice and looked as if she would stay a glorious eighteen forever. In the morning heat, she tossed a half-eaten persimmon behind her near the lotus pond and unpinned her wavy hair so it cascaded down like a magic carpet. When she disappeared into the *sarang baang* that was now Seongwon's art studio, he followed. Already, Seongwon was exploring.

Eunkang wheeled toward his studio, then stopped herself. So what if he was her husband? She would not descend to the pathetic tirades that she associated with her mother, who had once triumphantly sent Eunkang's father to jail under the adultery law to punish him. She thought of the girl's lavish locks of blue-black hair that picked up images like a mirror, and her blurry smile that made Eunkang think of sex. She dusted off the persimmon and bit through its hard, bittersweet skin, and imagined what she tasted was the girl's boldness. Monogamy was unnatural, Seongwon would say, and Eunkang agreed in theory. But in a country where female grooming was an art form, her own pageboy haircut and boy's hips and chest made her look more unconventional than she was. As sadness filled her, she covered her wide-set eyes with her free hand as if guarding her secret self from others. She willed herself into the stone in Yu Chi-hwan's poem, a stone so enlightened it was never moved to grief. It was unmoved by the chaos around it, so it could not be overwhelmed by anger: *Even if I were broken in half, I wouldn't make a sound.*

Eunkang and Seongwon had literally bumped into each other ten years ago at the Sheraton Walker Hill Hotel, where they were meeting potential marriage partners that their parents had arranged for them. Eunkang's *matseon* was with a man who listed his entire extended family's educational background (impressive), his salary (more impressive), and the optimal number

of children (two boys, one girl, preferably in that order). He made
it clear that her age was alarming and, in truth, made her unsuit-
able for him, all this before their coffee had arrived. She left him
to his pronouncements and eavesdropped on the more interesting
conversation near them; the stranger's startling, earnest metaphors
and hands as free as ocean squid seemed to frighten his date, but
intrigued Eunkang. She told her *matseon* partner why he would
remain unmarried, then escaped to the hotel lobby and waited.
When the earnest stranger emerged, she made sure to swerve into
his arms. He didn't look surprised, and instead said, "I know you,"
with a tenderness that made her wonder if in their past lives they
had loved each other. He was the painter Seongwon Han.

"A steel magnate for a father!" Her mother beamed. "I'm so
proud of you."

Her father said, "He's a promising painter. You'll make a powerful couple."

But the couple talked of art and freedom. Eunkang understood Seongwon's work as a dissenter because her father was a
democracy movement poet; Seongwon was excited by her open-
ness to a sensual life without children, inconceivable to other
women he knew. Eunkang, married before she had experienced
her first kiss, did not care about money or family reputation or the
infinite calculations involved in marriage. She had only trusted in
a vision of happiness.

In the afternoon Seongwon shuffled over to her studio in a
plain ivory *hanbok*, the very vision of humility as his pantaloon
legs swished and brushed the floor. He gazed at her new experi-
ments, *seoyang*-style, using oils: a wall swallowed up by moss, a
child confronting an F-15 Eagle's shadow, naked women with

heads shaved like monks. Critics called her work "beautifully detailed, feminine miniatures." She believed they were mistaken. In response to his look of a child caught stealing, she made her own grief comic by clutching at her heart.

She said, "You've been out corrupting the innocent?"

She worked to keep her voice light. The world was much larger than her small sorrows.

Seongwon began to paint the Chinese characters for her name, Silver River, on *hanji* paper. She dropped a lit match into the wastebasket, then tossed the painted characters into the flames. The paper curled as Seongwon watched, horrified. He desired in women the same scope as his art. His brushstrokes were more bold lines of energy than ink; he used new materials like horsehair and rice grains and reinvented two thousand years of *dongyang* painting. She, too, felt her breath harden at the sight of a beautiful young man; she wanted to wear shirts that showed the wild berries of her nipples. But all around her was: A man needs children to come home to. Too much education is unattractive in women. A lovely miniature.

She rescued Seongwon's work. It was a painting. It was her name. She pressed her face to its charred edges and inhaled the smoking *hanji.*

Seongwon kissed her forehead, her toes. His eyes, bright with worship, sought her approval. Was he a good enough man, artist, lover?

"You smell exactly like a woman should," he said.

"And you smell like you've been with a woman."

"That's impossible. I showered." He sniffed himself. "I smell like barley soap."

She maintained a careless smile to show that none of this mattered to her. "You always smell like women."

"They say there's a transvestite bar in Itaewon." He moved restlessly across the room and back as he referred to the neighborhood dominated by American soldiers. "We should visit."

She burrowed into his armpit and breathed in his accumulated disappointments that equaled her own. She had loved Seongwon's risks for greater freedoms, but time had done its work and now they lived ruled by the former dictator's cronies, and Seongwon had retreated into smaller, more manageable desires. Only then she had been shocked by her capacity to love all that was broken and flawed about him.

"Can you imagine?" His voice was eager, searching for something else to believe in. "A bar full of transvestites in Seoul of all places."

"Would they be safe with you around?" She kept her voice light. She refused to act hysterical, needy. She refused to act like a woman.

They made love; they made up. She tried to make their lovemaking, still affectionate but no longer exciting, more interesting for herself; she insisted on experimenting with different positions while on top. She looked down at the scars across his chest left by beatings in prison, his face now stripped of its confidence. How vulnerable he seemed to her in private, how boyish, so proud of his scars, his risks. His father was powerful; the government had let Seongwon live, but she was careful not to remind him of that. Soon she concentrated on herself. After a time, she forgot about the man underneath and she focused on her pleasure, until it was over.

He sat up and kissed her buttocks.

"I haven't washed," she said.

"I love every part of you."

She touched his receding hairline, masked by his shaved head. With the negative *ki,* that energy drained from her body, she was at peace, for now. When he made speeches, his eyes sought her calm presence. He walked bullishly ahead one day, then woke up at night sweating and yanking at invisible wires pulsing across his body. When she held him, he whispered, Thank you for saving me, into her ear. She had been trained all her life to take care of men, so how could she turn away from him, a man who needed her so much?

So this was marriage. With Seongwon, Eunkang had been allowed to be herself. She had thrown occasional chunks of cement at the riot police, she had worn obnoxious colors. While friends strategized for their children's education and labored under weekly visits to the in-laws, she neglected dirty dishes, and painted with no pressure to sell. They had not had children, and now never would, no matter how it grieved her. Marriage, free and fluttering. She liked that image of herself, untruthful as it was.

Seongwon was also himself. Too much himself.

The next morning, while she cleared the breakfast table, a bell rang through the *daecheong,* the main hall.

"It must be the help," said Seongwon.

"Help?"

He rocked back and forth, heel to toe. An excited reaction she recognized.

When Eunkang crossed the courtyard and opened the gate, she recognized the girl from yesterday.

Mina Lim, as Seongwon introduced her, was a beauty—the artist in Eunkang could not ignore this. Her face, bright and alert, diminished the garden's ginkgo trees and surrounding mountains into a mere landscape. And there was an uncompromising look to the defiant tilt of her hip, the way her generous chest jutted out in challenge, an independence that Eunkang occasionally glimpsed in the streets of Seoul. She was fascinated because she had never met these new generation women; most women, young and old, still played the desired types: the submissive, the unfailingly polite, the beautiful virgin. The type that Eunkang despised yet found herself imitating.

Seongwon's eyes roamed from Eunkang to the sky, then darted to Mina's tanned skin with thinly veiled pleasure.

"Hearty, isn't she?" He gazed at her as if admiring a Jean-François Millet or a Park Su-geun painting. "A real village girl."

Hearty, Eunkang considered, did not describe Mina's lean suppleness, like a silk streamer unfurling in the wind, or her full lips and large, fierce eyes softened by a curtain of lashes. Seongwon observed Eunkang, perhaps anticipating a scene. She would not give him that kind of power. She said, "Yes, that she is."

Each studied the other. Closer, she saw that Mina must be older than she'd thought, maybe twenty-five. Her distinctive scent of sweet rice and persimmons filled the space between them. Finally Eunkang looked away.

In the *daecheong* the doors on all four sides had been raised and latched to the ceiling, so the garden merged with the house. Mina's gaze wandered across the pond to the original sutras of

Monk Wonhyo and handcrafted furniture. Her gaze was rapacious. She looked at the room the way she looked at Eunkang, stripping it naked in one glance. Her eyes seemed to take in each item, calculate its worth, see through the couple's pretensions. Then she smiled, a sweet, surprising smile. Eunkang saw again the extravagance of their sleek *hanok,* and their hollow claims to freedom from attachment. How ludicrous were all attempts at defining the self! So what if they tended daily to their garden and cleaned their own house, activities that few in Seoul with their means participated in. In the village, elderly men carried forty kilos of rice on their backs. Many families still used outhouses.

"Seonsyaeng-nim." Mina called him teacher. "Your house is— a work of art."

Seongwon quickly—too quickly for his leisurely drawl, said, "Mina paints, too. My very gifted apprentice." He could not disguise his pleasure.

Eunkang played hostess. "And have you lived around here all your life?" No answer.

"And your family?"

Mina looked away. "In Seoul somewhere," she said. Though respectable women lived with their parents until marriage.

"You're starting to sound like the *angibu,* with all their interrogations!" said Seongwon. There was impatience in his voice, as if he expected cooperation with his latest game.

"Just being social," Eunkang said, meanly satisfied with the girl's discomfort. But there was also curiosity. Her first encounter with one of her husband's lovers, and she found herself disturbed, titillated, imagining Mina the way Seongwon might.

The girl would understand and flee, Eunkang guessed, most

would, and she was intrigued when Mina stayed. When Seongwon fretted about the mess and important Hong Kong art dealers
visiting in the afternoon, Mina merely said she would start with
the floors.

So Mina scrubbed. And Eunkang dusted. Seongwon's hands
fluttered like birds' wings as he made over-the-top pronouncements such as "It has to be so clean they can eat off the floors."
When Mina looked amused, Eunkang wished she could explain
that Seongwon was still intact, suffering beneath his self-
importance, and say that he was not like Eunkang's father yet,
corrupted by the respect accorded the elderly and the worship that
the public lavished on him. Of course she said nothing.

Only when the bell rang, Seongwon ran out of the house, his
hands pulling up the legs of his trousers as if he were wearing a
long skirt.

Eunkang wiped sweat from her forehead; Mina scrubbed one
corner of the room, radiating coolness as if her entire body was
water itself. Eunkang sat and kneeled forward, her knees tucked
under. She was attracted to the girl's sexual territory, the beauty
that reminded her of the old Joseon dynasty pleasure paintings:
the *hanbok* skirt flipped up, revealing a bush of hair, the *yangban*'s
body twisted around and into a woman like an embroidered
knot—those erotic paintings that made her feel more prudish
than she wanted. She found her hand reaching for Mina's shoulder. It was like marble under the rough cotton. Was this where
Seongwon had touched her first, on the round curve?

Mina stepped back, her face white with alarm. Eunkang
tucked her hands behind her, holding her brazen hand.

"The refreshments," she cried, and fled to the kitchen.

By the time Eunkang returned, Mina had been replaced by men in suits. She was left alone to adjust the air conditioner, to serve the finest ginseng tea. Where are the chrysanthemum rice cakes? Seongwon asked. Where is the fruit? As she served the men, they were so absorbed in their conversation they didn't bother to look up for more than a brief nod.

While the three men sat in lotus position on bamboo mats, Seongwon explained away his paintings as if he were teaching an art appreciation class. Quickened by his attentive audience, he laced humorous anecdotes into his careful, erudite observations. He seemed pleased, protected from the greater disappointments in his accrued knowledge and achievements. Eunkang sipped tea and marveled at how her husband had become more attractive to the foreign art world because now he was literally a tortured artist—he may have lost his faith and his confidence in prison, but suffering for the democratic cause had undoubtedly increased his market value! For most of the afternoon, the men, expecting a feminine public silence, did not address her. For once she was pleased to be left alone to her thoughts.

After the guests departed with their purchases, Eunkang told Seongwon that she needed to visit Seoul for the evening. He did not have to accompany her, for it concerned family-to-family negotiations for her youngest sister's dowry.

And though she flinched as she lied, he only said, "Send the family my greetings. Your father—I miss him." Since the elections, there was no longer a need for late-night organizing.

He became quiet. When she backed the car out, it nearly hit a strolling rooster. Village boys returning to the rice fields pointed at the black sedan the size of a small tank—yet another ostentatious gift from Seongwon's parents to embarrass Eunkang.

It was dusk by the time she made inquiries and found information leading her to a traditional *panjatjip,* a tiny hut located just outside the town limits of blue-slate roofs and rough cement-walled houses, where a girl of Mina's description was said to have recently moved in. It was one of those abandoned huts in the countryside that would have invited squatters who fled the city during the student movement: its wooden gate was missing its front door, its walls were made of dried-clay brick mixed with cow dung, and its roof of rotting straw was caving in. One last crow still sunning on a nearby telephone pole glanced at Eunkang. Within the gates, the *madang* bare of foliage was too small for a child to lie down in.

There were holes in the white papery screen of beaten tree bark; Mina could not have lived there very long. Eunkang slid the screen door open. She had a right to this much. The smell of freshly cooked rice, persimmons, and Chinese food washed over her. As her eyes adjusted to the dim light, she took in the room's permissive neglect. The room was an obstacle course of magazines. There was a sink of dirty dishes, a thin rack of clothes— bar-girl garments to support herself, Eunkang saw at once. She picked up a nightgown near the door and sniffed its damp sweetness, touched the clutter of sketches and tubes of paint, photographs, beads to make jewelry. A girl who liked making things. Her eyes moved to the canvases stacked against the wall. Of course, it must be the paintings she had come for.

The door creaked.

"What are you doing here?"

Mina pulled a string from the ceiling, then the room flooded with light from the naked bulb that dangled between them. Her body was squared as if ready to fight. The girl's frank beauty surprised and touched Eunkang the way beauty always did.

"Is my house your tourist attraction?" asked Mina.

"And my husband, yours?" Eunkang's own honesty embarrassed her.

There was nothing more to pretend. Still, Mina smiled that sweet, girlish smile as if determined to enjoy this.

Eunkang filled a kettle with water and green tea leaves as if it were her own house, then set it on the portable burner. She sniffed. "Chun Mee tea from China," she observed. "A little sweet."

Mina watched sharp-eyed but did not protest.

"My mother calls my life a tragedy," Eunkang said. "But she says all women's lives are tragic. Do you think it's so tragic?"

Mina shrugged. "We're just here for a little while, then we go. I don't think about big words like *tragic*. It seems so melodramatic. Our country's so melodramatic."

"So that's what's wrong with us!"

But Eunkang agreed with her. Someone else had watched the great, important men do their dance, and laughed, knowing that the magpies would continue to fly and defecate whether people lived or died. Knowing that in a mere hundred years, all their differences would not matter.

She poured tea and respectfully handed a teacup to Mina with two hands.

Mina accepted it, her head slightly bowed.

"You're very attractive," Eunkang said, and immediately felt mortified.

"That's a strange thing to say just now, but thank you." She set the teacup down at the corner of the low floor table, pushed a sketching pad aside, and sat down on the floor. "I never imagined he'd call me while you were there, so I froze. I don't do things like that, really. All I remember is cleaning!"

Eunkang sat across from her. "And now you know the kind of person I am."

"In Seoul I take good care of myself, not like this," Mina said, her hands busily defending herself as she made large gestures at the sagging tin roof. "I'm good at taking care of people."

"I wanted to know these things about you," Eunkang said. She dipped a finger into the teacup, let it burn. "To see you the way my husband knows you." She said this as if she had followed a plan, though she had surprised herself by coming.

"*Does* he know me?" Mina said, and laughed. "Why do you let him do this to you?"

"Why did you?"

"When you're gone for the weekend, the village kids use a ladder to climb into your yard and play." Mina smiled, amused. "They say they even watch your television. They're so afraid of you two, they put everything back exactly the way it was. Now that's manners."

"What are you trying to say?"

"I don't know," Mina said. "I'm a little nervous. I wanted to learn how to paint from the best. It was something I wanted to do, just now."

She looked up, bright-eyed, though there was aggression in the smile. She added, "And I guess I wanted to know what it tasted like. Power."

"And what did you learn?"

She considered this, cocked her head, and spit out, "For some people, floors have to be so clean people can eat off them."

This made Eunkang angry, and uncomfortable. It also delighted her. She curled up at the foot of the bed like a cat, while Mina sat on the floor Buddha-style. They loosened up because they had nothing to hide from each other; they would never meet again and were safe in that knowledge.

"You won't be surprised, but I've done some terrible things," Mina said.

"You're so young, how terrible could they be?"

"Terrible, and more terrible." Her head tilted proudly. "But I don't regret anything."

"I've never kissed anyone before marriage," Eunkang said. "That I regret."

Mina drank tea and nodded and listened.

"I wanted to be liberated, a new woman, but I lived so quietly." Eunkang spoke honestly, the way she rarely allowed herself, like a woman hungry for speech, and she felt herself lighter with each sentence.

"I would like a quiet life," Mina said. "My life's never been quiet."

"Would you be good at that, a quiet life?"

"My mother wanted a quiet life somewhere, anywhere. She wanted to be taken care of and be loved." Mina swirled the teacup, spilling on the floor. "She grew up around here. I wanted to see it for myself."

"I've always wanted to be a mother," Eunkang said. "I've always wanted children."

She stopped there, unable to continue. Only then Mina came closer, filling Eunkang's eyes with her long arms and breasts as large and round as a foreigner's, a body that had been raised on milk and meat instead of vegetable roots and rice, a body that would remember peace more vividly than it did the fear of war, the body of a woman the daughter she would never have might have grown into. This beautiful woman took Eunkang by the shoulders and kissed her on the cheek, like a real daughter.

"I'll be leaving tomorrow," Mina said decisively, mercifully. "It's time for me to go home."

"Where will you go?" Eunkang studied the way Mina carried her power. Would her daughter have been so bold, so sure of herself?

"Back to Seoul. That's where they are, the people who love me."

Only when Eunkang rose and asked to look at Mina's paintings did the girl become shy.

Mina said, "It's just me, dirtying up the canvas."

When Eunkang turned over the first canvas, then the next, she saw that the critics would say the work was amateur. Perhaps they were right, but she also saw how playful the paintings were, and how dark. The thick oil surfaces were sculpted, scraped into an age that seemed to date itself from the beginning of time, and the amorphous figures rising from that darkness that could be about creation, survival, or destruction, she wasn't sure. *I have seen,* the paintings said, and she wondered what it was that a girl of Mina's age must have seen. She had expected to confirm that Mina could not compete, and win something back—her pride, her dignity. Instead she was delighted by what Mina might be capable of someday, and relieved. There was also a sense of loss, which made her feel older than she was.

"Don't listen to what they say about you," Eunkang said, her voice vehement as if "they" were specific people they both knew. "They're usually wrong about everything."

Mina smiled, brightly this time. "It's a clear night tonight," she said, her hands to the windowpane. "You'll be safe driving home."

Eunkang allowed herself one last slow gaze, memorizing, before she shut the door behind her.

She drove rapidly home without decelerating, only stopping once when between two mountain peaks, a view of the moon, the vast rice fields, and the shadowy mountains stilled her with their imponderable gaze. She walked gingerly down the neat aisles of rice shoots and murky water up to her ankles and listened to the music of groaning frogs that made her feel erotic, sexy. This was her, finally listening to her body whisper its needs; she heard the woman she had imagined herself being. She took off her blouse and bra, tied them around her waist, and let the moonlight and the wind caress her chest and hard, cold nipples. With her eyes closed, her face upturned, she relived the persimmon splitting against teeth and smelled Mina's room in her hair. Someone might see her; she did not care.

Seongwon met Eunkang at the gate. He said nothing of the lateness of the hour and did not comment on her muddy beaded slippers and shirt, which only now she realized she had put back on backward. Instead he said, "Have you had rice?"

She shook her head, no longer pretending she had visited her family.

After a few minutes he reappeared from the kitchen with a

low table heavy with rice, soybean paste soup, beef ribs marinated in honey and soy sauce, and pickled vegetables. There was her favorite *banchan:* beef-stuffed chili peppers and candied lotus flower roots. Men rarely entered the kitchen; the store-bought *banchan* arranged on small plates was his usual plea for forgiveness.

"I made dinner for you," he said.

As she sat on the floor and ate his lie, he watched, delighted. He kissed her on the throat, the earlobe, the mouth, until she said, "That's enough."

He kneeled on the bamboo mat beside her. "I'm a foolish, weak man."

"I know."

"I want to be the universe for you."

She tapped the thin fuzz on his scalp with the fat end of the chopstick. "That's impossible."

She thought of Seoul, the city that she loved a new city now, with no more enforced curfews and now with young women talking too loudly in orange drinking tents with the men. The tear gas that had fogged the streets for the last decade was the past, democracy was theirs, and the riot police were now restationed as sentries by serious embassy gates and the presidential compound. The hundreds of thousands of protesters had nothing left to risk and nowhere to go but back to their own lives. They had returned to the disorientation of light conversation, weighing the watermelon per milligram at the market, waiting in traffic, enduring living and loving, like Seongwon, like her. So how could Seongwon be an entire universe when he could not even be a stone?

She blew air into his serious, devoted face, making him blink.

"It's hardly fair to place the universe on your shoulders." She felt wonderful, weightless. "You're so earnest. You take life so seriously."

"Have I disappointed you?" He looked worried. "I am disappointing, aren't I?"

"Silly man that I adore," she said, and kissed his baldness.

"What if a woman does what she wants and they call her a bad mother, a whore?" She pulled her blouse up to her rib cage and twirled her finger around her naval. "I like the word *whore*."

She said the word *whore* out loud again and enjoyed Seongwon's fright.

"The carp," she cried. "They'll look so beautiful in the moon!"

She scrambled up. He followed her out the door, determined and sincere. The carp now flashed an archaic beauty that reminded her of the traveling *pansori* singers and the medicine men of her youth who had all but disappeared. When she dipped her fingers in the pond, a large orange carp nibbled on her fingertips. Goodbye, she thought, to all the beauty around her. Tomorrow, she decided, they would return to Seoul, to home, and she would find out what other kind of life she could live in the city.

"I see Sagittarius." Seongwon squatted behind her, his lips to her ear. His voice dipped anxiously. "Oh, and there's the rabbit on the moon. What do you see?"

"Me?"

She broke away from him. She turned squarely and saw the man she loved, a man incapable of change. But she could.

"Seongwon," she said. "Wait and see."

THE BELIEVER

For jenny, *G* was always for God. God was there, God was everywhere. She saw Him in the penumbra of her father's doubt and her mother's anger plummeting out rust red. She saw Him in the vast, ululating dreams of all the people she met, and the nebulae that she sometimes woke ecstatically to, a monster gliding along the sea's black floor, traveling tirelessly despite the weight of human catastrophe, its prehistoric face the face of all time, the face of God.

Then one day God was nowhere. That day, she had come home from the seminary that she attended despite her father's desire for a doctor or lawyer in the family. She remembered hearing the gurgle of the yellowed refrigerator that they had bought used, and feeling thirsty. After slipping out of her sneakers, she went to pour herself a glass of orange juice. She hoped that her mother remembered to buy the pulpy kind, though most likely she wouldn't have.

That was when Jenny saw an arm in the sink, the small hand outstretched like a mast. A friendship bracelet circled the wrist. She saw the torso of a Chinese American boy she knew, a fifth grader in the neighborhood, protruding from the industrial-size waste bin. The Transformers T-shirt. The boy's pinkish-blue eyelids pinched shut, as if they had been forced closed, his dark lashes fanning out against his cheeks.

She closed her eyes for a time. It was the creation of her mother's mad rabble, one of her fits, Jenny told herself, but when she opened her eyes, the boy was still there. It was so humid the windows were steamed up with condensation, but she shivered. Only then she noticed her mother squatting in the corner, still holding a bloody saw that she must have found in the toolbox; she looked frightened, bewildered. Jenny felt a sudden hatred for this woman, but she was her mother—and how could you hate your own mother? She heard moaning and realized that it was her own sounds.

"Calm yourself," she whispered. "Calm. Yourself."

The sound of her breath was an underwater sound. Only the thought that the boy had a mother and a father who loved him kept her from running. Her feet moved millimeters at a time. They were so heavy, she thought, this is how prisoners' feet must feel. Finally she pulled the boy out of the bin, and, while her mother watched, cradled him in her arms. The top of his head touched her chin; she buried her nose in his hair's minty shampoo and sweat to suffocate the other smell, as she dragged him into a triangle of light and laid him across the tile. Blood now streaked her white T-shirt, her skin of milky pear. She stripped off her clothes, trying to feel clean as each garment dropped away from her. She wiped the blood rising from his severed arm with her blouse. Slowly she ran it down his shoulder's length and his pale, stained chest. The sun beat down on them through the narrow kitchen windows. Her nipples stood erect as if it were cold. She arranged the dimpled corners near the boy's lips with her still-clean pinkie so he almost looked peaceful. With her long skirt, she shrouded him. Naked, she kneeled in the pooling blood and, for the last time, prayed.

Her father refused to talk about what happened. Once her mother was institutionalized, the media uproar about "the Korean killer" quieted, and the hate mail from the local community had dropped off, he reopened a clothing store near South Williamsburg in the winter of '86. They moved away from Flushing. In their new neighborhood of Flatbush, he jogged block after block between cars while listening to vocabulary tapes; he remembered his customers' birthdays, even the ones who stole from the store, then tried to resell him the very same items the next day.

But there were small betrayals: his tidy professorial look gave way to hair like tangled grapevines that Bacchus would have envied; his teeth browned from forgetting to brush.

Thirsty for somewhere else, he began spending his free time watching Korean soap operas and playing a screeching music he called *pansori,* whose words Jenny could not understand. He began telling Jenny they never should have left. On the day of his twentieth wedding anniversary, she caught him lying in a mountain of her mother's lingerie, his nose in the 34B cup of a bra, his hand folded around the crotch of a lace panty.

"You look so much like your mother," he said as he gazed at her waifish figure.

As for Jenny, she felt like an intruder in the home she had found in the church. Where had God been that day? she asked herself. What had they done to be so punished? She quit the seminary she had just entered; with her family's new notoriety, her presence seemed hypocritical. But then her father would politely ask, "How was church? How was school?" She did not want to worry him, so she did not correct his assumptions.

Instead she furiously walked the city in dresses resembling togas, for she did not approve of many modern practices, including painted-on jeans and fitted T-shirts. Still, men ogled her skin that burned at the slightest sun, her straight black hair under a sun hat as wide as an extravagant sombrero. That day a man with the crotch of his jeans to his knees tugged at himself and said, "Babe, you can suck my blood anytime." She gave him the finger, giving herself a small thrill, and walked faster. Canal Street. Chinatown. Midtown. She stalled at the entrance of a church, but was too afraid to go in. Most days she forgot to eat. She returned home exhausted to her father sitting on the sofa waiting up for her, the way he had done for her mother. Once, when she returned home, he put his bare feet up on the table by his dinner: caramel popcorn straight from the microwavable bag, a plate of spicy radish kimchi, apple juice. She watched him from across the room; they might as well have been as distant as Flatbush and Seoul. He made room for her in front of an evening soap opera, and for the first time since her childhood, she smelled the acrid undertone of rice whiskey on him.

"My lovely daughter."

He made two pigtails with her hair and tickled her cheeks with their bushy ends.

"Appa," she said, "how can I help you?"

She wanted so much to help him.

"How lovely it is to have a daughter," he said.

As she used his shoulder as her pillow, Jenny wished she could pray and make their lives intact again, but when she closed her eyes, she saw the boy. Then she could not pray. Her father, who had prayed only for her mother's sake, pretended not to notice. All the while, she felt God leave the orifices of her body. The being who had been her life force now kept her at a distance, so she regressed into the person she had been before His grace: a battered sliver of weed in the chaos of the universe.

A year went by. It passed like a silent movie. It felt like a long sleep.

One day in August her father showed up at breakfast, his ashy color restored to peach. He twirled a round fish cake between his fingers like a cigar.

"Pack a bag," he told Jenny. "Today's a special day."

"Where's there to go?" she asked.

He said, "Good daughters don't ask questions to their parents, they listen."

"Then I'm not a good daughter," she said. But she was happy to be anywhere with him.

Within an hour in the Daewoo sedan, shouting over low-flying airplanes, he told her that they were driving to see her mother.

"You tricked me," she said, which was not exactly true.

"It was a surprise." His forehead creased up the way it did when he was annoyed. "Don't you want to see Omma?"

She sat erect in the passenger seat. She did not want to see her mother, changed as she was.

She said, "Of course I do."

"You can't pretend you were born out of a hat," he said. He reached out to ruffle her hair, then stopped.

The rows of maple trees blurred as the car accelerated. Green highway signs for Trenton flashed below an awning of clouds. She could see it now, the careful planning. In the suitcase, dried squid strips, her mother's fuzzy sleeping socks and eye mask, the waterfall music on CD she refused to travel without. As if they, mere mortals, could waltz in and rescue her. As if a visit could restore her father's stolen happiness.

The ward for the criminally insane was as sad as plastic Jesus souvenirs. No matter how festive the more enterprising guards tried to make it—doilies of turkeys across the window sash, a headdressed Pocahontas taped to the door from last year's holiday season—it was a prison for the afflicted. Jenny walked closely behind her father, avoiding the corners of the waiting room that were round and soft, like a used bar of soap. Even the front desk officer had a wandering eye that made her look as if she had been around sickness for too long and had become infected.

Her mother, called Helen Nam in English, Heeyoung in Korean, and now case 6479274 in the ward, was sitting cross-legged behind the bars like a lady. Her chin dragged in the air as it lifted, a beautiful, broken motion. Her mother's eyes wandered shyly to her and looked at her—really looked at her. It almost made her mother human to Jenny, but then her mother's face shifted away as if embarrassed to be seen. That was it. Her mother disappeared, unable to bear herself anymore, and began rattling an invisible tin tray, smacking her lips as if sucking off a bone. She became again the woman with blood on her sinner's hands.

Behind a window of Plexiglas opposite them, overlooking the small room, a nurse yawned.

Her father's gray eyes were narrow, fierce with longing. His hands gripped the bars as if he were about to rip them out. No one else was in the room, for him.

"Dangshin . . . how's my *gonju*?" he said.

Behind the concrete wall, Heeyoung's head dropped and revealed her black hair growing in bluish white, then she haughtily lifted her nose in greeting.

"Hi, Omma," Jenny said, but she choked on the word for *mother*.

"Jenny-*ah*." Her voice was as light as spring rain. "It's Jenny, right? It's been too long, I almost forgot. How long have I been here?"

"A while, Omma."

Her mother collapsed back into her seat. She rocked precariously on the chair's edge, her eyes black splinters that absorbed the light around her. She was there but not, Jenny realized, as if murder had changed her and made it impossible for her to return.

Tugging at her hair, her mother seemed exhausted by speaking. Once again the meds had fogged up her world. She spoke slowly, each word a strain on her slowed-down brain. The air, cleared of the din of dim voices, must have become a void of depressing silence.

"Say it," her mother said. "You're laughing at my—my ball-room ruins."

"Omma . . ."

Her mother's hands made figure eights in the air.

"I have visited heaven. Yes, I have been with the Lord. My dear, what am I saying?" She struggled, trying to concentrate on Jenny. "You are going to church, aren't you?"

"Every Sunday," Jenny lied.

"Make sure you take Daddy with you, or he'll go to hell," she said.

"Yes, Omma."

"Remember when I took you to museums?"

Jenny nodded in encouragement. Her father pushed her away and pressed his face against the bars.

"What can I do for you?" he said. "Anything, anything," he said, as if this were possible.

Her mother touched the bars between them. They looked hungrily at each other.

The guards and nurse averted their eyes. Jenny thought of the boy in her arms and gagged. A boy who had knocked on their door selling newspaper subscriptions and had been mistaken as the devil. Her chair fell back when she stood up.

"*Geejee-be!*" her mother screamed at her, banging her wrists against the bars, bird wrists that looked incapable of harm. "How can you wear my face? You stole my face!"

Her father picked up the chair, scraping it upright. He began cajoling her mother through the bars as if she were a child. "No one's sick in this house," he had said when she used to sob in bed all morning. "Your mother is not sick!" he had said until he couldn't.

He turned to Jenny. "Careful," he said.

"I have to go," Jenny could only say. First Corinthians 13:13. *And now these three remain: faith, hope, and love. But the greatest of these is love.* But now there was a dead boy. There was her mother, a murderer, and Jenny, incapable of mercy and love.

"Don't go," her mother said. Her hands made gauzy gestures in the air. "Come back, *uri* baby. I'll be better, I promise."

"We can make her better," her father said, and hit the wall with his palm so hard it trembled. "They've made her crazy, crazier here. Just listen to her."

"I'm listening," her mother said, and a trickle of frightened laughter escaped her. "But I never hear anyone but me, singing."

Jenny and her father took turns driving past tract homes as ugly as soggy toast, stretches of strip malls with parking lots big enough for a dozen cemeteries, then empty northern roads. They drove as though they were being chased by the story of their lives. As if they were afraid of their dreams, they did not stop for any sustained sleep. He had begged her, please. He never begged, so they were returning to Las Vegas, where the family had spent their first year in America, husband and wife working at a swap meet, as if they could start over again. But two days later in Colorado, just beyond mountains that made the Appalachians look like molehills, he finally parked at a bar cockily called The Bar. A deer and her fawn stared at them, then picked their way up rocks and disappeared in the fog.

"I'm too young to drink, Dad."

"They won't care. This is nowhere."

He skipped to her door and opened it as if the car were a carriage.

They sat at the bar that was dressed up like a gloomy Victorian drawing room. The wall's wainscoting was chipped and the bar's worn varnish grooved with the marks of fingernails and coasters. Behind the bartender, there were bottles of liquor and a wall of postcards of other bars and other parties. One of a man in leather jeans with two girls, a brunette and a blonde, in his arms. Other places that were always better than here. Her father ordered a brandy sour. He had not shaved for days; his eyes had darkened to slate. Jenny drooped onto the counter, her head propped up by her thumbs. What if they had fit into the order of things? Would her mother have become as sick as she had? Immigrants. Indeterminate and silenced.

Her father was darkly determined, and plumbed his second brandy sour.

"This place is riffraff." She swiveled on the leather stool. "Bird shit."

He stared at her.

"Young lady, watch your language with your father. Your God up there may be watching."

"God is always watching," she said, hoping it was true. "He would want you to stop drinking so damn much!"

It felt good to see his shock, to feel him press his hand hard on her mouth until she promised not to speak that way again. Then he drank.

"I wish I could believe again." His voice was detached. "I wish it were all true, your God thing. I wish I knew how to."

She began humming a hymn, a melody of grace as he began drinking again, hoping the words she used to believe in would restore him. *As the deer panteth for the water, so my soul longeth after you* . . . But she stopped; she did not feel God in the room.

Her father sang "Aeguka," the Korean national anthem, over the jukebox. He clapped his hands as his voice became louder, a sentimental vibrato as he seemed to escape from his adopted country. He was asked by a Latino man sipping a piña colada to keep his voice down. Her father looked at the stranger with hatred, as if he were facing the very men who had, at different times, bashed in his storefront window, drilled through the roof, and made off with the family's livelihood and, eventually, his wife's health. The man was twirling a paper umbrella between his work-worn fingers when her father adjusted his shirtsleeves and, with a sharp swing, punched the man off the stool.

Several bruises later, her father checked them into a motel somewhere in Colorado. He was rumpled, confused.

"How's your head?" she asked.

"It's there," he said.

His eyes did not meet hers; instead he inspected the green velvet curtains, their fabric wafting of gas passed after yogurt, the bedspreads on each twin bed that featured mottled brown versions of a Civil War battle. The room smelled of preserved duck eggs.

He said, "There's no alarm clock, air-conditioning, or shampoo. Funny! Someone even walked off with your Bible."

Jenny looked up, annoyed.

He said, "There's nothing here."

"What you did at the bar," she said. "There was no love in it."

But she was also tight with judgment of herself. Love, it was the greatest challenge.

"I've told you a dozen times already." He jabbed at the dry air. "In the bar, it must have been allergies."

"Appa, you hit a man." She sat on the bed, legs crossed. The woolly bedspread prickled her awake. "For the hundredth time, it wasn't allergies."

"With some allergies there's a swelling of the brain. Your personality changes." He sat on his bed and folded his arms across his chest. "I've read about it."

"Where? In the *National Enquirer*?"

"It wasn't me," he repeated. "It was allergies. It's true."

"I'm eighteen, Appa. You need to find your way."

"Why should I find my way?" He picked at a loose thread in the flat sheet. "You saw her. I saw her. She's gone, forever."

She fell backward onto the bed, her face now to the ceiling that was exposed and unpainted, the same sallow yellow of her mother's face that had seen too little sun. She jumped up on the bed and touched the ceiling.

"What am I going to do?" His jaw was slack. "Nothing's going to change with time. It's as if our life never really happened."

She wanted to pray for him but prayer was now beyond her ken.

"Appa," she said, "I've lost a mother, too."

They began to cry together. They were quiet as the year that had passed filled the room.

"This is undignified," he said. "Everyone back home would be satisfied, in secret. That's the way it is, you know, when you leave the country and fail."

She hugged him, patting him on his back, then his head, as if to bless him with a power she didn't have.

"Who cares, Appa," she said. "It doesn't matter what anyone thinks." But God.

She woke up at night slick with sweat and her jaw clenched so tight her molars hurt. She must have been talking in her sleep, asking for forgiveness. It had happened before.

On the bed next to hers, her father sputtered sighs. As his hands glided across the comforter, she wondered if they had shared the same dreams. She moved to his bed and held his hand, trying to comfort him. When his sleep became even, she went to the window. The only living thing outside was a panting Labrador with its tail stiff in the air like a weather vane, rubbing its sex against a truck's hubcap. The glass frosted over with her breath until the dog became a horse. Her mother was leading it, the enormous horse, the way she had once imagined it into their living room until a younger Jenny, too, had seen its liquid eyes, its steaming breath.

"But you're not even here," Jenny whispered. Still, the images resurrected themselves, the way that her mother's way of seeing had always haunted her. The wild punctuation of her mother's sentences penetrated her, and through the motel's double windows, Jenny saw her mother's body wrapped in a metal corset and naked from the waist down, tiny seraphim grimacing as they licked her with their bruising holy tongues. She touched the windowpane. As the rough tongues bathed and burned her mother clean and made her body sing ecstatic with a song so pure it was silent, Jenny reached for their compassionate light. But when she ran out into the courtyard, there was no light to baptize her. There was only a dulled moon. Only a chicken bone under her foot and the dog looking sore from its rapture.

She went to bed again, but sleep was impossible. So she stuck her head into the refrigerator (the room's only working appliance) to wake herself up. "Hello, Old Gin," she said to the quarter-full bottle that her father had somehow sneaked past her, and unscrewed the cap and drank it, coughing, until the bottle was empty. "Nice to meet you, Mr. Moldy Orange." But when she blinked, the orange became the boy's head. She pulled back. "Get out of there," she said. But it stayed where it was.

She returned to bed. She lay, her arms rigid at her sides. When she closed her eyes, there was Janus, two faces looking to the past and the present. A strip of rainbow emerging from pine trees, a gliding Boeing 747, a landscape of miracles. Her eyes flew open. There was her mother.

Frantic movements came from her father's bed. She sat up. His pants were pushed past his thighs. One of his hands was navigating himself back and forth as if sprinkling a lawn with water. Between pauses he ground his teeth. He was still asleep.

She felt horror, shame. But there was something else. A desire to touch him, to give him back the man who had swallowed a fistful of American soil on his arrival to the strange land, to show where he now belonged, to restore the woman he loved to him, but she was only a human being. The corridor lights created stripy shadows across his face and made him look mad, delighted. A man forging his own heaven. She should leave. Still, she stroked the rise and fall of his modest chest, the ridge of chest hair that divided him. How long it had been since he was loved.

The touch moved her, warmed her in the darkness the way that only love could. Her hand descended. In the conviction of alcohol, the desire to give back his stolen happiness, she reached below for him. Between exhalations, his hand stroked her hair. When his hips rose, she moved her hand faster. His sleep-breath fluttered with happiness. All the time the prayers that had been lodged in her throat deluged out. She prayed for her youth, her dreams, for her faith to be transferred to him. She prayed for Lot and his incestuous daughters, for their sins. She prayed for grace. For forgiveness. For her father's happiness. By now his hands had pushed up her nightgown and pulled her into a strad-dle on his stomach. They tugged down her cotton panties with his thumbs, but slowly, as if asking a silent question. His eyes were now open. She raised one leg, then the other, leaning like a dog, and let him find her mother in the folds of her flesh. Soon there was nothing between them but their body's salt and sin and the endless longing. She lowered herself until his heat warmed her breasts. As his lips closed over her nipple, she began to cry. Appa, Appa, she whispered, as they were purified, washed in the blood of the lamb.

Then she finally saw Him. She was so relieved to be back in God's presence that it didn't matter that her eyes and nose were bleeding and her face was peeling off, and her throat scorched from the light and heat of Him. He parted the buildings for her, the steel edifices as flexible as paper, so she flew through the air that raised up enormous collared preachers and men with ten-gallon hats and strippers with metallic dots over their nipples, past the growing black night that devoured until she was in the thunder and the rain, with the ancient sand of the Sinai Desert whipping into her eyes and ears until they were driving with the map He was drawing in her head that would lead their family to salvation. And they were making good progress, until she realized that they were going nowhere at all, and that the rain was coming so fast that the car, no, the bed, floated down the pavement past the Joseon dynasty lacquer wedding chest from their living room, her father's Webster's dictionary and his sets of leather-bound photo albums, the rattling kitchen sink, her mother's Peter, Paul and Mary LPs, past the squeaking front door, past her own porcelain figurines of Abraham, Noah's ark, Mary, and the manger cast swallowed by water. And finally there he was, baby Jesus the size of a thumb, bobbing on the water's surface, drowning valiantly like the rest of them.

In the morning over pulpy IHOP pancakes, they read newspapers. The more plates clattered, the more cordial they were to each other. After her father ordered extra crêpes, he didn't complain when the waitress, so high she couldn't have told trout from filet mignon, returned balancing Hawaiian pancakes with pineapple slices scalloping their edges. Nothing indicated that they had changed to each other.

"Would you like more syrup?" he asked, and poured maple syrup on Jenny's plate until her pancakes were soaked.

"I'm sorry, I'm sorry," he said, and dabbed at their soggy centers with napkins, then realized what he was doing.

"I'm sorry," he repeated, and swapped their plates.

He leaned on his elbows as if he could not support his own weight.

She moved her food around to the plate's edge. She couldn't eat. The pancakes she cut into wedges fit for a bird's beak.

The same waitress's big Texan hair sidled up. She slapped down the check, exposing an upper arm punctuated with needle marks, then stood beside the table and waited.

Her father put down exact change, then an average tip.

The waitress's lips moved as she counted.

"Can't you give me another buck?" she said. "I'm down on my luck."

"Miss, you forgot to ask us if we wanted anything more," her father enunciated as slowly as a language audio tape, careful not to make a mistake. He looked past her as if he were now thinking of something else. "And what happened to filling our coffee cups?"

"Hey," the woman said. "This isn't some fancy restaurant."

"Do I have to argue my tip? Well, then, you didn't bring us our crêpes," he said with the same indifference. "And rubber tires are more tasty than your pancakes."

The woman looked confused. She rapped the table with her knuckle and said, "That's the meanest thing I heard all day."

"I'm sure you're a very nice person," Jenny said. "He's not usually like this."

Her father looked sharply at her. His mouth was a thin line. She looked away.

"I am." The waitress's head bobbed up and down. "It's been hard."

Jenny added a ten to the bills. It was as soft as tissue paper in her hands.

Her father crushed his napkin into his coffee cup.

"The tip's more expensive than your pancakes," he said.

"You're a good person," said the woman.

He stood up. "She's a sacrificing—fool."

Finally, Las Vegas, a city where a decade ago, they had believed. Hotels glittered, the fountains were spumes of white foam. They drove past a gaggle of Asian women trotting after a raised flag; these women carried buckets for slot machine coins and had on white gloves as if they were attending a golf tournament. In a pink limousine, a shadowy woman licked her fingers, a gremlin of a girl stuck gum in her own hair. They pretended to be absorbed in everything they passed, even the strip joints advertising Colgate commercial models and Miss America finalists. Anything not to look at each other. As they drove, the glitter they left became the green of a suburb that abruptly became a thirsty land fissured with cracks. An eagle circled their car twice, dived, and throttled a roadrunner, a roadrunner that would crack open the neck of a scorpion. The decomposition and derangement and damage that the living and the dead inflicted upon each other—it, too, Jenny now understood, was God's country. It was also the country of fast-food franchises.

The McDonald's where her parents had taken the family for their first American meal together was designed as an enormous Happy Meal container. Ronald was painted on one side holding hands with Mayor McCheese, with his other hand waving in the air as his crew of kids headed up the capitalist's version of the road to Oz. An impossible, perfect happiness.

"It's still the same," her father said, his voice wondrous.

As they passed a sculpture of Ronald McDonald by the door, he ran his hand across Ronald's plastic hair.

Behind him, Jenny found herself doing the same.

They joined the queue of minorities, single parents, and bulky men and women who looked to have gone through a lifetime of Big Macs. Her father watched them as if he were standing at a great distance. But outside the window, Jenny thought, beyond the fun house decor and forced cheer of the Happy Meal box, someone was committing suicide, someone was grieving the murder of their son or daughter, someone was enduring God's endless tests. The thought connected her to a vast web of strangers, and their confusion and hurt became hers.

They ordered, collected his Big Mac meal and her chicken salad, and slid into a glow-in-the-dark orange booth. He tucked a napkin into his collar and began eating.

Behind them, a girl as round as a pincushion made bobcat

sounds. She made certain that she would not be mistaken for any other animal by screaming, "I'm a wild bobcat! I'm a wild bobcat!" between leaps in the quivering booth.

"You were a strange child," her father said. He squinted, as if seeing a detail from a time long past. "Fasting, praying. You used to draw little crosses into your rice. Every Sunday you had to go."

"What's going to happen to us?" Jenny asked.

He put down the Big Mac. Crumpled up his makeshift bib. "I should be the one jailed."

"I wanted it," she said. She could not look up. "I wanted to be with you."

"It's all I've been thinking. What kind of family have we become?" His voice sagged. "Happy luck I'm not Christian, or where would I be at the end?"

"Appa, God forgives His sinners." She needed to believe that this was true.

He stared out the window to the stretch of blue desert road.

"I'm sorry you look so much like your mother."

The girl jumped on the trampoline of her seat, spinning the pinwheels in her hair.

"Mommy! You're not listening! You're not you're not you're not." Now she sang, "I'm a baobab tree."

"I'm your father, Jenny. I'm an animal. Worse than an animal. The devil, that's it." His head dropped in his hands. "It's unforgivable."

"I made it happen."

"You're my daughter."

"You told me about how women in the Joseon dynasty married at thirteen."

He looked up. In his eyes she saw how it was for him, to be in a world without hope.

"There's nothing left in Las Vegas." He stood up. "This is nowhere, too."

Eighteen, and she felt older than time itself. *For all have sinned and fall short of the glory of God*. Romans 3:23. God must still be there, somewhere, for all of them. She bowed to the table, weeping, one hand across her mouth. She moved across her father and her shame, across the customers and the entire tribe, strangers to one another, all the way to a woman in her lonely cell, whose cries were another kind of prayer.

BEAUTIFUL WOMEN

U NDER HER MOTHER's skirt, there is the shimmer of pink gills. Mina strokes the down of her mother's leg past the puckered marks of slugs on her mother's thighs, up to the dark starfish she spies under a strip of translucent fabric. But these mysteries become ordinary, merely thighs and fatty flesh, when her mother slaps her hand.

Mina crawls out from under the bell curve of her mother's skirt. The guest, with eyes as green as liquid detergent and fuzzy hands, makes his goblin's smile. His entire body is one green uniform, and underneath, his hide of hair is thick, luxurious. The only thing he ever talks about is a Nam, the same Nam that her missing father is very friendly with. Will this stranger beat her with his club? Or with it bestow on her a cave of gold? She does not like to show her fright, so she sits on the chair with her legs dangling but crossed, like a grown-up.

Tell me a story, she says to her mother. And waits for her reward.

⟨

Her mother muses, her mother mulls. Her mother gives her a
handful of chocolate tears wrapped in silver foil. Should it be the
one about the evil brother who steals the good brother's fortune?
Or the one about men who turn into oxen? She looks flustered,
her forehead creases with frustration as it sometimes does, when
making decisions. When it is so simple! Finally, she asks, in her
pleading voice, What does my princess want to hear tonight?

You spoil her, says the man, breathing out menthol and cigarettes. She doesn't act seven.

I *am* seven! Mina says, and comes out from under the table, so
he can see her full height. I'll be eight soon.

She's lost a father, Mina's mother says, which sounds like *fahder*
when she says it. She becomes sullen, no longer interested in him.

Mina seizes the opportunity. Tell me a goblin story, she says.
She stares at the stranger's eerie green marbles. He folds his pink
hands neatly on the table and stares back. How can her mother
trust a man who irons his collar crisp but overlooks what must be
dirt and moss under his fingernails?

All children like animals, the man says. When he smiles, he
bares glistening yellow teeth.

⟨

Hana has decided that everyone will like the new student Mina.
When she announces that they are now best friends two days into
the spring term of 1971, no one in the third grade, not even Mina,
dares challenge her. Hana is too big for age eight, too certain, to
contradict.

At lunch she sits down by Mina, her body as bountiful as her personality. Her eyes open to the size of spoons when she sees the wheat sausages and rice Mina will eat for lunch. Angered by all inequality, with a flip of her sturdy wrist, she releases the metal clasp to her oversize lunch box: rice, kimchi, preserved radish, fried anchovies, fried squid, eggs, and beef marinated in soy sauce. Her large hands gesture out to her lunch box like a traveling *pansori* singer's fan. She says, I give you half this universe.

⋌

At home it is impossible to see Hana in her mother's fat folds of flesh that smother with each hug. There are only the skirts of her mother's stiff silk *hanbok* scraping against her cheeks. She says, My little genius! You're as good as any of our boys.

Mrs. Song's professions of love echo as loud as threats. They are so pronounced that her voice shakes their yard cloistered by four buildings, clatters the crocks of preserved foods, and breaks through their fortresslike gates down to the Yeongdeungpo neighborhood's serpentine alleys. She is so loud that the barber stops shaving his customer, a tabby cat springs toward the sound, and Mina looks behind her as the uniformed pusher pushes her mother and her onto the crowded tram, pushes them all the way in.

⋌

Soon after Mina and her mother, Mrs. Lim, or Sergeant Brown's woman, as the foreign community has dubbed her, arrive at Namdaemun Market, her mother pretends to inspect crates of mackerel heads. She does not want to be seen hungering for imported banana clusters by their old neighbors. The tropical fruit cluster is nearly worth what Mrs. Lim made in a day working at a laundry service near the U.S. army base. I won't listen to their insults again, she says, and tugs Mina hard into an alley, where spools of thread and buttons to dress entire nations are sold. Her panic reminds Mina of what she already knows: if it weren't for her birth, her mother would not have to run away from anyone.

So what does Mina do? She runs.

✦

In the Itaewon neighborhood, this is what they had said: *GI's lover. A blackie's bitch.* The chortles bandied about by the neighborhood's old-time Korean residents just loud enough to trail after the family.

They had smirked hello after Mina's father, Sergeant Brown, persistently greeted them after church with his brisk pace and friendly black face, his determined smile, like his stepdaughter's, intact unless he was asked about his family in the United States. Then he would stop smiling and say, "That's none of your business." When there were no witnesses, the Korean congregation snatched away their children by their armpits and would not let Mina play with them. They gossiped about the noises from the house, not knowing that when Sergeant Brown was drunk, he tickled Mina or her mother; they did not know that he wore bifocals that divided his eyes in half, read three newspapers each morning, taught Mina how to read, and had been trying to secure a long-distance divorce from his first wife (a vengeful woman!), and always deferred to Mina's mother with, Yes, my dear, as if it pleased him to lose to her. They said it was God's will when Sergeant Brown left to fight in Vietnam; their faces twisted into grimaces as they searched for someone else to judge. How confused the neighbors were after Sergeant Brown died in action and the Lims moved away from the house near Yongsan's U.S. military base, a trail of turquoise butterflies fluttering after them.

ᚷ

Mrs. Lim is calling for Mina somewhere in the labyrinth of Namdaemun Market's crates of spoiling vegetables and fresh pig's heads, but Mina forgets this as she wanders through stalls of fermented mackerel, dogs hanging by their hides, jars of alcohol with snakes coiled inside, army uniforms and canned baked beans smuggled off the army base, and 101 varieties of pickled vegetables.

Lost, she swerves into an ancient man in a horsehair hat and bumps into his cart of squirming squid, hops over a rat sniffing into the mouth of a blowfish, skittles past naked mannequins and stuffed tigers. When she feels fear, she pinches her thigh to distract herself.

Boys don't cry, she says out loud. Spring's first dandelion seeds flit across her nose and make her sneeze.

You lost, little girl? says a shopkeeper with the white whiskers of a mouse. His face softens as he gazes at her.

No! she says. I'm never lost! She impales him with her glare for noticing.

When he hunches to her height, she runs, with her companions from her favorite folktales: the garlic-eating bear, a pipe-smoking tiger, a fox shape-shifting into a beautiful woman. Mina is a warrior with a quivering bow, an iceberg, a tortoise barricaded in his gunmetal shell; she is invincible. She is almost as brave as her father. But an hour later, she is alone, zigzagging from alley to store to escape her shadow.

⟟

What a beautiful child! the dried pollack vendor exclaims after she nearly steps on the sleeping girl's egg-shaped face. Mina, the size of a sack of rice, is prostrate beside boxes of body-scrubbing cloths. Her cheeks bloom with a garden of color, her two pigtails of hair curl into question marks. Disappointed by the two sons the vendor has raised into ingrates, she dreams of taking the girl home and dressing her up in yellow ruffles and bows. Maybe even parading her loveliness on one of those newfangled black-and-white machines called televisions. In her trance, the vendor leans to snatch the girl up in her arms, but is too late.

The girl's curtain of eyelashes flies open, revealing the ambers of her bright, friendly eyes. She says, Have you seen my *omma*? and yawns with such a stretch of her arms that her top jacket button pops and rolls across the alley's pavement.

⟟

After Mina has been warmed by the smoky coal grate and tucked into bed, Mrs. Lim trundles through yet another market and buys thread and buttons in bulk. Soon, she thinks, as she passes women carrying wooden A-frames loaded with fabric, women whose cracked, lined faces have been ravaged by their hard lives, soon I will be one of them.

✦

The fortune-teller, the closest thing Mrs. Lim has to a friend that late spring, sniffs her as soon as she enters. Smelling the bowl of home-brewed, milky *makgeolli* that Mrs. Lim consumed before arriving, she says, Mrs. Lim, you've been drinking.

Mrs. Lim digs into her tumultuous purse, sprays herself with a vial of lilac. She says, How can I not drink when I'm afraid of my dreams? Each night she imagines what must be her man's toothless jaw trying to speak from under Vietnam's jungle. The rusted clutch of some booby trap around his feet. The gobbets of his brave flesh stuck in camphor trees. He was a good man, and she had imagined another life for them, another country. Now she fears her family's bad luck is following her; she has had fortune with her dreams.

The old woman squints, and knits her painted eyebrows together. She mumbles, War after war after war. They're bleeding our continent. She fumbles with her book of numbers and reconfirms Mrs. Lim's time of birth, day, month, year. When she opens her mouth to speak, Mrs. Lim says, I never wanted to go back to the family farm; I wanted to be somebody. And now it's the end of love, the end of guarantees. She raises her enameled nails beseechingly. So don't deny me. Still, after several apologies, all the fortune-teller claims to see in the numbers is the ruins of time. A time of money and of speed, though men and women dare not hold hands in public, a time when people do not ask audaciously what is happiness. She says churches will protect the dead and the living, the country's people will rise and be crushed by the government, and time will swallow up Mrs. Lim's beauty.

⤝

The government's swallowed up my son! Mrs. Jang shouts at the neighbors. She has taken to standing at the street corner, railing at passing pedestrians. Her nineteen-year-old son has disappeared; tears the size of salmon eggs squeeze out of her eyes as she curses the government. Her diffident husband, afraid that she, too, will be arrested, pulls timidly at the flaps of her sleeve.

Give me back my son, she says, and lifts her husband up by his shirt. She stands outside until her shoes are worn away by June's monsoon rains. As the fierce summer heat sets in, her wringing hands become leathery in the sun. Her dark hair turns hoary white out of grief, her brown eyes fade to gray. Mina, Hana, and the other kids in the neighborhood slow down, listening, as they pass her on the way home from school. Sometimes they bring her a few rice cakes or a bowl of leftover rice porridge from home, as their mothers instruct them to. To the curious children, the only ones unafraid of her grief, Mrs. Jang relays her story of how the black-suited men took her son away because he had been seen handing out political pamphlets.

Which of you reported him? she demands.

I didn't report him, Hana says, so upset by Mrs. Jang's tale that she shivers in the white heat. I promise.

Everything he said is true, Mrs. Jang says, as her anxious husband tries to pull her back into the house. You've made him disappear for telling the truth.

⤝

Across the street corner from where Mrs. Jang spends most of her days, the mini-mart keeper washes dishes and sweeps for his wife, gives her back rubs, and makes all the women envious. While Hana hides in the aisles, Mina watches Junho, a boy in their third grade class, fishtailing across the mini-mart floor. His face is ecstatic, a fleshy plum. Mina barricades herself behind an aisle of shrimp chips and bags of rice crackers as tall as her, her large eyes lit like tinder, her grip a tourniquet around a tin of tuna. Someday, she vows, she will resist Japanese colonists, fight in wars, come back a war hero, be equal to the boys.

Mina, here I am! Hana's voice calls from behind packets of dried cuttlefish, as Junho heaves like the rough East Sea, rubs his body up and down against the blackened tiles. It is the first time Mina has ever seen him smile.

↜

When their parents have completed the honor rituals to their ancestors and are sleeping off the Lunar New Year's feast, the neighborhood's children try to catch the moon. One of their fathers said that the Americans have learned to walk on its cratered surface, so they are determined that at least the Koreans will be the first ones to catch it. Hana will buy the successful boy or girl coveted silver-foiled Hershey's chocolates off the black market; Mina has promised a kiss to the victor. The moon looks so close. It seems entirely possible.

Boys take turns releasing the swing and gliding as high as they can. Girls jump from the top of the gleaming slide and fling a fishing net into the sky. Still, the universe is too large, and they land, dusty and defeated in the sand. Within an hour the seven of them line up on the chilly bench, somber with disappointment. Junho, the oldest by three months, says, I knew it was impossible.

The youngest at seven, a girl so poor she was once caught eating leftovers from a garbage can, begins to cry. She casts a fistful of sand at him, and makes the sky cloudy for a moment.

Mina kisses the girl. Of course it's possible! she says. Here it is! And pulls the net over Hana's solemn moon-shaped face.

⊀

Mrs. Lim is convinced that the moon looks more beautiful in other countries. Look, she says. Look how ugly our moon is. And as she holds Mina up, she makes her daughter reflect on its dishwater color, its streaky gray surfaces.

⊀

While Mrs. Lim searches for a new moon with the green-eyed man, Mina tells a story. Though the outdoor toilets used by the tenants smell like winter's roasted chestnuts and ammonia, the number of children grows in the neighborhood's kitchen-size playground.

Mina stands on a plastic horse, her feet sway in the pink stirrups. The kids facing her sit on one another's laps, on the swings and slide, expectant. Jungsu, who tries to touch everyone's butt while laughing; Eunhee, a girl with no eyebrows and skin so pale it looks bleached; Gyeongjin, a boy who once tried to share a chicken bone in his mouth as a gesture of love; a gaggle of older girls who like to braid Mina's hair and dress her up in their outgrown clothes; and others. The only one absent is the one that matters most to Mina: Hana, locked up on a Saturday afternoon at an abacus class, with her brothers.

Mina waves her wand, her mother's bamboo spatula. The

wind bites her nose and ears red, lifts her hair, and transforms her into a witch. She waves her wand again and casts her enchantments.

The audience is listening; she is ready to begin.

↤

It is there, it is real, when Mina promenades across the playground, her head high. They see Mrs. Lim with rose of Sharon growing in her hair, from her shirt, from her very toes. The girls lean forward, entranced as Mina walks delicately across the pit of sand.

Where are you going? they ask.

To Texas, of course! she says, naming her father's hometown, where he had promised they would live someday after Nam.

Why Texas, they say, when our country's the best in the world?

Over there, she says, now curled up in the woolen lap of an older girl, houses are built for giants, and families use walkie-talkies to talk to each other. One cow is big enough to feed the whole Korean army. And there's never any winter!

A few more minutes of this, and the children are convinced that Texas is where they want to be. But when they ask her how she knows so much about America, Mina remembers that she is supposed to keep her father a secret, which angers her. She begins to act out the way her father will escort her mother back to the neighborhood that evening. There will be, she promises, a red-and-green palanquin with silk ornaments dangling from its four corners. The kids are breathless, their eyes straining to see this man that no one knows anything about.

They watch the tongue of the alley, waiting for the fans made of peacock feathers and the wood-carved marvel carried in by the four assistants that Mina has promised. They wait, the tips of their toes and ears white with cold. They wait and wait, but no palanquin comes. Still, no one remembers this when with the wave of Mina's wand, snowflakes fall into their hopeful palms.

⨍

When Mina wakes up in darkness, the smell of rice wine curls off her mother's breath and surrounds her like a fuzzy blanket.

Tell me a story about my father, Mina says. And waits to be dazzled.

⨍

Don't ask me about your father, Mrs. Lim says. She twists off her wedding ring that Mina insists she still wear, at least at home, and holds the gold band up to the ceiling light. Her smooth face sags as she tucks her chin in; it is the size of a raindrop in the band's reflection.

She says, I've told you and told you again. He's not your real father. And he's dead.

But he is the only father that Mina remembers. The portrait of the man that she has grown up with has been turned over; she turns it upright so his wide almond-shaped eyes and his white teeth gleam back at her. Somewhere off the grid of the picture are his large brown hands and the glowing brown shoes that she likes to stand on top of. Her mother says he has gone from Nam to heaven, but Mina refuses to believe that he will not return to Seoul.

Don't cry! Mina says, her face deep in the folds of her pillow. If you don't cry, he'll come back. Why are you crying?

I'm crying because I'm sad.

Mina is an unsympathetic nine-year-old. She bolts up, crosses her arms, and says, You shouldn't bring strange men to Daddy's house.

⸙

The shouting surges from the bedroom at sunrise and continues past noon. In the refrigerator Mina spies a tub of dried anchovies, puffed rice, a plate of dried cuttlefish, and leftover fish egg stew. No real food, no creamy chocolate milk or hot dogs, none of the foods that her father used to produce from brown paper bags. She lies flat on the floor and pushes around in a protective circle while listening to the enemy's voice barrel through the door. Something is thrown, broken. A slap, a scream. *You think you're the only woman in Seoul?* the man with sunflower-colored hair says. Then her mother's voice: *I knew you were another American, too soft to fight his own wars alone so you make our people go.*

You think anyone wants this war?

Mina chants her hand into a bamboo wand, commanding the cuttlefish to change into Hershey's chocolate, for the shouts to become a song, but all that transforms is the door now gasping open and the man's bare toe, a raw ginseng stump that reminds her of a goblin's lump, boring into Mina's rib cage.

⸙

He is Mina's avowed enemy, the slouching American soldier with eyes as green as sea grass who has begun appearing whenever her mother sings, I'm lonely, I'm so lonely, over breakfast. He calls her mother the shirt lady because he picks up his laundry from her every week. He says it unkindly. He has her father's stubble of hair but not his kindness, and a laugh gloomy with the war living inside his organs. Nam this, Nam that, is how all his sentences begin. Mina wants to meet this Nam.

Her mother's hand is over her jaw, swelling an apple red. On her neck, a cut the length of a razor blade.

Mina knows what to do. She bites the enemy on his hairy arm just over his shirt cuff, imagining beef marinated in soy sauce, crunchy chicken's feet, as she sinks her teeth in as far as she can. So far, it will hurt for him to pull on a sweater. With one hand he twirls her up into a merry-go-round as her mother watches. Crazy as Mommy, he says.

My daddy will eat you for this, Mina shouts, though she was four years old when her father left home, and cannot remember what his voice sounds like anymore. She swerves out of the enemy's grip. Her fists become a goblin's club, but still he says, You're old enough now, Little Miss Mina, you pretty little fool. You think your daddy's coming back for you?

⚹

Since Mr. Kwon has returned from Vietnam at the war's end, his son Junho has begun stealing coins from kids younger than him. He kicks and scatters jacks across the dirt road when the kids play, although he had revered the game a month ago. His legs below his shorts are laced with belt-strap marks.

What if your father had never returned? a friend asks him one day.

Junho's face, as long and bleak as a Goguryeo warrior in comic books, brightens. Then he wouldn't be here now, he says.

↰

What shall we do about Junho's family? As lotus lanterns are being strung across cables from street to street for the Day the Buddha Arrived, the neighborhood's women ask themselves this. They admire the paper lanterns swinging above their heads, and share stories about the disturbances coming from his family's house and how they have seen the oldest boy and his little brother out on the streets playing at midnight, at their age. *Did you know his mother's having an affair with the local electrician? That's centuries-old news. They've been seen in sheds, cargo trucks, when the lover can't scrape up the money for an hour in a room somewhere. Do you think the man pays her?* They know that Junho's father drinks away the grocery money as he flounders from bar to bar, trying to erase the war images that no one wants to talk about. All have grown up in the ruins of the Korean War, all have suffered. But this is a new Korea. The city has risen from the rubble, there are jobs for anyone willing to work six days a week, so long as you ignore the sudden disappearances of outspoken citizens. There is even money for the revived citywide Buddha's Birthday lantern parade! No one wants to talk about yet another war.

↰

When the green-eyed man stops making his stealthy visits, Mrs. Lim takes Mina to wander through the corridors of the department store. It is Sunday afternoon, and some of the best-dressed women in Seoul have gathered at this church of fashion. Mina dashes around, furtively touching the pyramid of Spam cans stacked in the center of the marbled foyer, their tinsel a towering symbol of modernity. Mrs. Lim watches the women trapped, moving inside the miraculous wooden boxes. They look so safe, she says as her voice breaks. They look so beautiful.

⤙

On the screens, remote women parade the perfect flips of their chignons, their bobs. Their black-and-white faces are more demure than the women Mina knows: the neighborhood's broad-shouldered, loudmouthed *ajeummas* who rummage the market's garbage for near-rotten stalks of spring onions and yellowing lettuce heads because they are free, and discard their dignity to work, feed, and clothe their families through the hunger years. When these women elbow their way down the aisle past the gloved bus-ticket girl, even the men are afraid of their forceful smiles.

These black-and-white women can't be real, Mina says decisively, and tries to find out by hugging the object of her mother's love. The electricity tingles through her hands and brightens her cheeks as she presses against all these wives, mistresses, heroines, victims (she must ask her mother what a mistress is) as she tries to enter the screen. And she almost succeeds, she believes, when her mother lifts her off the ground with a cloudy frown and dangles her, and says, That's very naughty of you.

I know you can't enter a television, Mina lies. She pinwheels her hair around a finger, trying to hide her shame. Oh why oh why can't she already know everything?

⊁

May I help you? A mannequin leans into Mina's view. The broad face is painted so thickly white that at each wrinkle, the makeup has cracked into rivulets. Mina leans, reaching toward the woman's cheek, eager to see how deeply her finger can penetrate, but the stranger snaps back to attention. Mrs. Lim misses all the excitement; she has withdrawn her best powder compact (made in France!), which she saves for special days, from a purse removed that morning from its dust bag.

Mina is appalled by her mother's evident inadequacy in this palace of handbags, but she does not know how to rescue her. To the saleswoman, Mina points her finger at the store's sign and says, Someday, we're going to live in a house as big as your store.

This charms the stranger into a smile, which seems strange to Mina, since the woman does not know her mother, so how can she possibly be happy for her?

What a good girl you are, and so lovely, the stranger says, and reaches to pat her, but Mrs. Lim pulls her daughter away and begins circling the department store as if she is an actual paying customer.

⊁

It is a perfect day when Mrs. Lim takes Mina to the zoo and insists that her daughter be allowed to mount the elephant. Mina rides around the ring, waving at the last remaining swallows in the bare trees. When she is helped off its hairy back, she says, I wish I had a granny to watch me.

Mrs. Lim is the kind of mother who says with a hard laugh, You know that's impossible, since I was born from an egg, like King Bakhyeok in the Old Joseon period. She doesn't explain how strange and difficult her family was; she remains a spontaneous miracle, a mystery to Mina, a mother who has arrived from nowhere. And because she is the kind of mother that she is, afterward she takes Mina to the movies for roasted silkworms and popcorn, and later that evening dresses her daughter up in a yellow princess dress and matching barrettes and lets her eat sweet rice cakes for dinner.

She is the perfect mother!

She is also a mother who, at the year's end, tells her daughter, In America every family is Christian and has a two-story house and Cadillac, and possesses more happiness than I ever will. She elaborates, though Mina is starting to wonder, Who are these Americans that live such gilded lives? She is a mother who, that Sunday afternoon, has her daughter kneel to pray for her father who is not her father, then for strangers: the conscripted Americans and the mercenary Koreans who have straggled back from Vietnam. The kind who tells her daughter afterward, You don't know what I've given up for you, then holds her and says, I'm sorry, I'm so sorry. Who, that night, cries when she mistakenly believes that Mina is asleep.

↟

Puberty, prepubescence, pornography. This lexicon of mischief could wake the dead. Mina, just turned thirteen, is learning what these words mean. So when a thirteen-year-old boy whispers the word *sex* in music class, the disruption is magnificent. The teacher soundly beats the boy who whispered the viral word. Still, Mina mines the forbidden word; the students look at one another and see men and women, and are darkly changed forever.

✦

You capture a hair, you capture a boy's heart, Hana says over lunch on the first true day of spring. She has found a short boy's hair (though it could be from another girl's bangs) hooked to Mina's ear. She inspects the sliver as her eyes, wide and as innocent as soybeans, brighten.

She raises it to her nose and inhales. It smells like passion, she declares. She says with envy, It smells like love, though she carries a tin *doshirak* from home with the best homemade ingredients, the most expensive art supplies, and shoes that she once confessed her mother shines every day for her.

Mina drops the hair into her tin cup of water and pulls her face long like a horse with her fingers; she doesn't care for boys or studying, but she loves to laugh. Sing the national anthem backward, syllable for syllable. Steal the teacher's glasses. Reenact her favorite movie scenes for friends. Play dead. It is late spring in 1975, and by now, the soldiers commissioned for Vietnam have returned and are living in indifference—to travel all that way to fight for the Americans, and lose, and weren't they paid for their services? That is what people say, but it never brought Mina's father back. A man who has become her secret to keep. A man to mourn.

Love, love, I'd rather eat raw squid for lunch, Mina sings in perfect pitch into her chopstick, trying in vain to stay uncomplicated and thirteen forever.

It'll happen to you soon, Hana says wistfully. I've seen the way Junho looks at you.

ᅕ

Junho comes and goes to school like an alley cat, ignoring the tolling bell. No wasted motions, no fat. A young, wheeling fury. Alkaline eyes. A mouth that does not know how to smile. Most of the female teachers, made timid by him, say nothing.

ᅕ

Adolescence has not been kind to Junho, Mina decides as she watches him sleep on his desk. His face reminds her of the carved masks used in farmers' harvest dances: an elongated shape, crudely drawn-in lips, pupils so black they absorb the classroom lights. He looks like a horse, and there is nothing worse.

They sit in polar corners of the room. Her chatter accompanies his angry silence. When she brushes hair out of her eyes, he flicks an eyelash off his nose. She fidgets throughout a chemistry exam; he sleeps inside the leaves of his comic book. If she catches a cold, he develops a headache. After the music teacher slaps him in class, she praises Mina for her singing voice. Mina thinks, We're nothing alike, but cannot stop watching him.

ᅕ

Alone girls are different. Jiwon tosses the cotton balls that flesh out her bra to the bathroom floor, Mija lights a cigarette—an activity banned for women, Gangin prays before she drinks a carton of soy milk; between classes, Mina jumps up and down in the bathroom stall to wake herself up. Outside, the Seoul sky smells of pepper gas and burning trash, but in the mirror there are only girls looking at one another, eager and afraid of growing into women.

꙳

The mirror in Mrs. Lim's room faithfully reflects misery and magnificence: a pyramid of her dresses, a nest of souvenirs, a portrait of Jesus hanging off a nail. A stopped wristwatch, a body's impression still visible on the cotton *yo* spread on the floor, the worn blade of a used razor, a cluster of black ants in the corner, the blood of a crushed mosquito staining the wall, Hana in her frilly bra and panties, and Mina, tottering, perilous in her mother's yellow platform heels, imagining the world looking at her.

It is electrifying to try on her mother's swishing satin skirt, her coat as long as a wedding gown, to imitate the way her mother's age and life story change each time she speaks. She imagines herself dancing with Jongpil; with Hyeongmin, with Junho. She imagines her father clasping her hand. It seems impossible to think that one day Mina will fill these shoes.

꙳

At Mina's house, Hana has decided that they should study each other naked in the bedroom mirror. She says with authority, We have to be as honest as rice cakes. So we can improve ourselves.

Mina's finger circles her own breasts, her curious artifacts that are half the woman her mother is, those indecisive lumps that developed before her classmates. Short, stocky Hana inspects her own chest. Hana, whose parents take her to Mozart symphonies. Hana, a girl who beats the boys in arm wrestling and bicycles with no hands and gets stomachaches when she doesn't complete her homework.

Mina's eyes are on the tiny nodes of life rising from Hana's chest. It hurts, doesn't it? she asks, her hand now on her friend's sweaty breast. Hana nods, turning up her full-moon face that smells of butternut squash, no matter the summer heat.

Mina points at the sock she has jammed down the front of her underwear, and strides across the room with the swagger of a military man. She points a finger down at Hana. Down here. She adopts a teacherly frown. This is where men put it. She knows this because she has spied, just once, on her mother.

Hana shrieks, That's where I go pee!

It's where the baby comes out, Mina says, her voice smug with knowing.

Hana said, Your breasts are beautiful, like an icy milk bar.

Mina squeezes them until they turn blue.

Hana's giggles bubble out past her hands. My mother wouldn't notice if I grew three breasts. She's so—so abstract.

Mina says, My mother's a nine-tailed fox. She drinks the blood of men. Like this, she says, and kisses Hana on the lips.

⼢

Mina's sallow breasts, her purple nipples ringed with budding hair, are bewildering protrusions. They are the same breasts that her mother scents with roses. The limestone and ocher of the Venus of Willendorf's most ancient breasts. The breasts that babies suck. The breasts that men love and Saint Agatha of Sicily cut off for her faith. Kannagi tore off one of hers to fling at the

South Indian city of Madurai, sacrificing her breast for a curse. The medical practitioner James Guillimeau, in 1612, believed that through a mother's breast, her body's imperfections transmitted to her babies. Parmigianino, Isoda Koryusai, and Pablo Picasso immortalized the breast. They are the breasts that Junho asks Mina if he can touch that summer, that will grow into perfect bell shapes. Mina does not see much in breasts. They are sore, they are impossible. That is, until Hana cradles one of Mina's breasts. They look like vanilla pudding, she says.

⟡

When a small protest against the president-turned-dictator Park Chung-hee flames up on the streets, Mina and Hana are in their favorite corner of the Namsan Library. They press their noses to the window and see the city center crowded with police surrounding a few foolhardy protesters. Will we ever go home? Hana says, shivering. Will we ever reach nineteen and enter college and vote?

Mina says, Of course. Though she isn't sure if she wants to grow up.

Mina ensconces herself on half the sofa with a book on Mars as if it is an ordinary day; Hana sits on the other half with a history book, but she flips the pages so quickly she cannot be reading.

After a time Hana says, Everything will be okay. We'll become judges.

Mina touches Hana's fingertips.

We'll change the court system.

Hana touches back.

We'll change the laws.

We'll be law professors!

They laugh.

We'll be—

What will you be for me? says a man, peering from behind a triangle of newspaper. He has gray eyebrows and a sharp, toothy smile. His hand is moving so fast that the sheaf of newspaper rustles, the print moves up and down. Hana hides behind her arms but Mina watches, fascinated by his joyful distress, until she feels herself inside the seasick letters, capsizing.

↙

Junho is afraid of his father. The sixty-two students in his homeroom class are privy to this because every month or two that fall, his father, the Vietnam veteran, stumbles in waving a bottle of *soju* as if it were the *taekguki* the students pledge loyalty to every day. Each time, Junho becomes smaller, his arms wrapped around himself in a protective lair. That day, his father comes waving paper, saying, Junho, your *gijibeh* of a mother's run away! Since his return he has never had a job. Everyone knows this because he is a morning drunk who sobs through the neighborhood housing blocks. He used to be nice enough, the neighbors say, then go back to throwing out the trash.

Mr. Han scans the room as if looking for his wife, then slumps into an empty chair. Even when the homeroom teacher stands as close to him as she can, he will not move.

Mr. Han, she says, how thoughtful of you. You're only interrupting exactly sixty-two students from studying.

He looks up. The only subject worth studying is the military, he says. Look at our president! I promise you, those strong-armed boys will keep this country going.

Students shuffle in their seats. One bold student whispers, Drunk *gaesaekki*.

Junho does not look up. He has become stone. A rock jetty.

Even after Mr. Han is persuaded out of the classroom, Junho stays marooned to his desk, his head slumped into a textbook. He lets out an occasional sound resembling a snort, but Mina understands.

✦

Teachers tell the students that they live in a democracy. That means, according to the present practice, you are prosecuted for criticizing the government. If you make friendly comments about North Korea, the police label you a Red and you are sent to jail. The authorities arrest you for appearing suspicious, which means you look like a union worker, an intellectual, or a student. The most dangerous activity is not skydiving but mobilizing. If you are male with hair long enough to brush against your shoulder, the police intercept you; students in Mina's class have seen two college boys sheared on the street. And the teachers! They demand thank-you money in envelopes from each parent and become rich. Everywhere placards read: DO YOUR CITIZEN'S DUTY. REPORT SUSPICIOUS ACTIVITY. Anyone can be a spy, Hana whispers at lunch, but who is the enemy?

✦

Teacher Roh is known to refuse the envelopes of money, an understood obligation if you don't want your child bullied or overlooked.

If you come to class two minutes past the bell, she beats you as you crouch with your buttocks in the air.

Chalk flies as she prints across the board. But when Teacher Roh turns, she catches Mina reading Hana's note. Mina crushes it into her mouth and begins chewing it like stringy dried squid.

Spit it out, her teacher says, and holds out her hand. Who wrote that thing?

She points at the class motto above the blackboard that reads: YOUR TEACHER IS YOUR THIRD PARENT.

In this country you have so many parents to pay respect to, from the president, the elderly who know what is best for you, your relatives, your teacher, your mother and father, down to your older brother or sister whom you call by their titles.

Mina swallows; she protects those she loves.

The ruler slashes once, twice, striping her cheeks scarlet. The students cramped against the back wall strain to look. Junho wakes up from his nap in time to see Mina smile.

Don't you dare smile, the teacher says.

But Mina is used to taking care of herself; she believes she isn't afraid of anything. She raises her chin so her smile is more conspicuous.

When her teacher goes to the desk for the rod reserved for boys, Mina flicks her tongue out at Hana; it is covered in purple ink.

⟨⟩

Junho comes and goes to school at will. Sometimes he leaves in the middle of class for a glass of water or returns with a snack. Some say he works several part-time jobs to help his family, since the government ignores the war veterans, for hadn't they volunteered and accepted American dollar bills? My mother said the war never happened, Junho says, but it's still happening to me, then hits the wall with his knuckle. Still, the teachers pretend not to see and do not wield their rulers or bats. How can they, when he has grown facial hair since the sixth grade? When he does not care what happens to him?

After school he snatches taffy out of children's mittened hands. Late at night he hauls crate after crate of canned drinks, gulps *soju* from the bottle. He sits and stares at the moon. He watches the sun rise with his eyes closed until his father finds him and drags his son indoors.

☇

Yet another night when Mina's mother is still not home, the shadows look like twenty-foot mountain rabbits with bristly fur and incisors the size of doors. You're not even tigers, Mina says, feeling five years old again. She could flash as many teeth as she can, and kick them in their swollen rabbit stomachs. Instead she thinks about Junho.

☇

Finally Mrs. Lim returns from a dinner held by a foreign church congregation member and dispels the shadows. Her hair is spiraled up like a western staircase, her face is as smooth as a Korean radish. Her hourglass figure is shrouded in a black wool coat. She holds her hands up helplessly and says, The only one who wants to marry me is Jesus.

What's so great about marriage? Mina says. Her hand aches as she pushes away a jar of peanut butter and reaches for her mother, a beauty that Mina cannot believe does not mean more to the world. But her mother says, Don't touch me!

Mina hides behind her palms as her mother tosses her purse across the room. Copper coins twirl across the floor, do their dance, then tinkle to a halting stop. Her mother says, I'm a mother with child. There will never be new beginnings for me. Do you understand that?

Her mother's gasping fish face, its terrible need for oxygen, makes Mina feel cold. Her body shivers with hurt. Her mother wants pity, but for once Mina cannot speak. She hides behind the peanut butter and stares into its terrain: plateaus, cliffs and craters, an endless, treacherous desert. She swirls her finger in, sucks on its creaminess. The sweetness explodes in her mouth. The kitchen light above is how she imagines the eye of God. Stickiness stitches her mouth together and holds in the anger and the sadness, as she waits for her mother to love her again.

ᛣ

Somewhere, fathers are bankers and mothers shuttle their kids to the sea. But here, boys blow up a frog to see how many pieces are created. There is camaraderie in robbing small shops at knife-point. An actress makes love to an amorous producer on the set, while a few respectful yards away, the staff waits; a few blocks away, a real estate agent advises sons and daughters on how to confiscate their parents' property. North Korea hijacks a plane. Men beat up their wives, their wives beat their children, the children beat their friends, and they all help Mina fall asleep to their nightly music. But even here, in the crowded subway, a boy sits on his friend's lap, a Buddhist monk makes music tapping on a gourd, a coin is found on the street, the dried pollack cart man sells his day's stock early, a couple touch each other all night long and forget to sleep, an elderly woman plants red peppers to make kimchi, and *Haam! Haam!* the groom's friends cry, as they wind through the chilly alleys carrying a pearl-inlaid chest with coarse silk, coats, and jewelry for the bride's family. Children play jacks with stones warmed by the sun, and everywhere there is the pungency of *bbeondaegi* and *soondae,* there is decency, there is happiness.

⼓

Mina visits Itaewon, where the American military men drink with paid women. Behind a large black man in green fatigues, she imitates his walk, imagines what it must be like to be his daughter. Her feet are so heavy with sadness that when he turns around and sees her peeking from a furry hat, she cannot turn away. He smiles, even laughs, and speaks babble in a friendly voice before he returns to his friends. She wants to say, My father who's not my father, they say he's dead in Vietnam, but there's no proof. But she no longer knows the right words.

⼓

All winter they have waited for spring, but now that it is here, the yellow cloud of Gobi Desert dust still mists windshields and makes everyone strangers to their own faces. Nineteen seventy-six is the season of freedom, as Mina's mother leaves for days at a time to be

with a male friend. The season of beginnings and of ends, as dictator cum president Park Chung-hee mourns his wife killed one year
ago by a bullet meant for him. It is a time of protest poetry, of
Hana's notes to Mina saturated in purple and yellow ink, of air
fragrant with cherry blossoms, of miniskirts that have the police
racing for rulers, and of fresh octopus still writhing on ice and *soju*
by the river in the all-night hum of covered drinking tents. It is a
time when North Korea's tunnels dug into the South are discovered, and South Korean fishermen are kidnapped by agents from
the North to study how the culture of their southern enemies was
changing. And red is everywhere, in the raids the police make to
uncover communists, in late girls squirming in the stink of their
first bloodied cloth napkins, in Mina's cheeks when the teacher
reads out the students' ranking, from the first, to Hana, who is
second, down to Mina's name, which follows the sixty-one other
classmates in grade seven. Mina had stayed up the night before the
first day of exams waiting for her mother's return from a prayer
retreat, so had fallen asleep during the test. Now she stoically takes
a public beating in front of the class. No one's remembered for getting good grades, she says cheerfully, leaning against Hana as she
hobbles out of class. Besides, someone has to be last.

↜

At last Junho gives in to the new boy's wishes. In an alley yards
away from the school they circle. Circling, the school's best reluc
tant fighter and the one ignorant enough to challenge him. Junho's
feline eyes, his skinny grace, give new boys false confidence. Junho
squints into the sun just above the blue roof tiles; he tenderly

plucks a sprig of purple daisies growing from a crack in a wall. Hold this, he says, and rests it on an underling's attending palm.

⤙

Students circle them, waiting to see if totalitarian governments can be overcome, if a new order is possible. They wait for Junho to whiplash the boy with his fist, or for the new boy to twist Junho's wrists back until they snap and have to be wrapped in a cast. Girls bet on how long the new lamb will stand.

The boys circle. The new boy thrusts with his predictable bulk. He misses and is punched in the gut. Boys stomp their feet. Someone whistles. When Junho's fists batter the new boy into the wall, Hana frets that this is such a waste of energy, but Mina wonders, How can you not admire Junho's lightning fists, the whip of his feet that move with medieval brutality? Junho moves casually in and out, transforming the road of potholes and smoky brick walls into his personal theater. That is, until Hana stands between the boys, determined to stop this endless violence. Her hands are raised like a traffic warden and her eyes dilated with fright, as she says, You'll have to hit me first.

⤙

One day in May with a sky as brown as sandpaper, Mina sings, Go home! to the schoolboys who pursue her. They just want to visit a tearoom with her, they shout, trying to look dignified as they run stiffly with backs straight and black school hats cocked to the right. Hana, tough and sweet with too many teeth in her smile, gasps, Can't we just meet them? I'm going to blow away with the

cherry blossoms. But Mina continues to run because she is really
a crane, at ease among the clouds, high above the city choking in
coal and industry.

↖

They backtrack the streets they know well past Chinese delivery
boys plying the sidewalks on bicycles; they flee through serpentine
one-way alleys that smell of its outhouses, past two-person factories cobbled together with tin and scrap wood and men with peb-
bly faces huddled over bowls of steaming noodles. Once the girls
lose the boys, they stop for snacks at a stall peddling boiled silkworms and spicy rice cakes on a stick for less than an *oshipwon*
coin.

If I were half as fast as you, Hana says, baring large, square
teeth coated in chili pepper. Mina laughs, and flaps her arms to
cool herself in the rising humidity.

If I were half as beautiful as you, Mina says. Nearby, a man
streams urine into the gutter, then flicks the last of it off with his
index finger. Such indignities sadden Hana, but Mina is too happy
to notice the ripening smell. She drinks red-rusted water out of
the community pump, then runs again because she is young. They
trample across the ancient city of Hanyang that is now Seoul, that
is becoming a maze of construction projects; they pass aged
women who have lived through Japanese colonization, a civil war
that smashed the country into two, and now the American presence and flushing toilets; they pass kids sucking on icy *jju-jju* bars
and boiled silkworms in paper cups, *panok* houses built of cardboard and tin cans of baked beans where entire extended families

live, then a shiny shopping mall. The girls' eyes are as bright as firecrackers, and in their breath grows a garden of roses.

≺

They dash along the main road and pass Mina's favorite local movie theater, pass a pork dumpling stand older than the girls, until they are stopped by a van plastered with campaign slogans.

Elusive local politicians predestined to win by ballot fixing have reappeared with their theater of megaphones, presents, and trinkets worth the cost of a bus ticket that middle-aged *ajeummas* in floral pants scramble for. Here are the politicians standing in front of waving banners and chanting, Remember number two on the ballot, or number four, their mouths like trumpets. The blood vessels in their eyes are inflamed, and their bellies cumbrous with dog penises and deer antlers for their libidos. From the tops of vans painted with campaign promises—LOWER TAXES! LOWER MILK PRICES! A SIX-DAY WORKWEEK! A HOUSE FOR EVERY FAMILY!— they wave their fat fists to the neighborhood's mothers. Their banners are held by men bowed so low they resemble dwarves.

None of them have hair, Mina says. It must be a political requirement.

It's wrong, Hana says. The lies they keep telling us.

Her fists are on her waist; she is furious the way she rarely is, her eyes darkened to ash with what they have seen over the years: stooped child seamstresses and demonstrators trussed together with rope as police baton them in the gut, a student dragged across the pavement by his bleeding feet. Before Hana erupts for her newest cause, her latest underdog, Mina pulls her by the hand

and runs, not knowing that all around them there is change and loss. This is a time of garment factories and of fear, a foreign time of blue eyes and flaxen hair. Villages are razed for progress and farmers become overnight real estate millionaires. It is a time of youth, and therefore a time for death, a time of silence as Hana yearns to speak. And because America is the most powerful country in the world, it is an American time while Mina's mother struggles to start over again, and Mina seeks magnificence.

↗

Finally she is fourteen, but all Mina worries about are the patchy stains across the wallpaper and the peeling green kitchen cabinets that Junho must notice. The furniture makes lumpy shadows in the light that is the same at three in the morning or three in the afternoon. It is what you do when the muggy summers are long and you are true teenagers at last. Mina mounts Junho, his hand advances up Mina's shirt, and Mina's traverses up his. They have watched their first porn film (illegal, they are everywhere), and they have reassured each other that they are practicing. Mina claims the male part (she will *not* be like her mother!) and she clambers on top, her school skirt flipped up. Her tights are rolled down. A cool trickle of sweat runs down her thigh. Her hand descends down his shirt to his waist. Junho dips his fingers into a small bowl of roasted seaweed and eats a few crispy pieces. Those same salty fingers creep up her skirt and explore her dark places. But the door opens, and Mina falls, tumbles off Junho's lap onto the floor. She tugs down her skirt.

Omma, she says.

Her mother's eyes go wide. Her hand hangs midair to her hair.

She says, It's not my fault. She shakes her head several times, begins unloading bags of goods, as if readying for nuclear fallout. Her frantic hands toss a packet of black beans across the counter as the clock ticks the hour.

⟡

Mina says, We were just playing! Junho says nothing. His leg shakes, her hands smooth down her school skirt. Their legs clamp together, waiting.

⟡

Mina's mind retreats from her mother. She longs to escape, but there is nowhere to go. How much has her mother seen? What have they been doing? Suddenly Mina abhors Junho's strong thighs, his eyes the faded gray of clamshells.

She smiles, slings an arm around her mother's shoulder. Nothing has happened; her mother has seen nothing. Just having a bit of fun, playing around. Because that is all it is. But Junho stands there, his hands patting his pockets, looking for cigarettes that he should pretend he doesn't smoke in front of older people. He watches them baldly, his eyes flicking over the bags of groceries, over each tender gesture. It is humiliating to be watched this way; she feels betrayed.

Mina's palms make petals around her mother's face, she kisses her on the nose. At fourteen, she has the kind of beauty that makes the local pastor blush. Male teachers pretend not to notice her as they watch to see who is watching her; the female teachers dislike her confidence. When Junho finally escapes without proffering a single excuse, Mina's hands flutter through the bags of food. She is charming enough, she is sure, to make her mother forget.

Finally her mother smiles. Her tired face stretches with fear, and longing, though Mina is standing in front of her. You never could stay still for a minute, she says.

↽

All men are dangerous, Mrs. Lim warns Mina as she paints her lips strawberry red, sets her hair into a quivering black beehive, and dons a geometric print skirt that flirts at her knees. But when she makes her entrance in the chapel, the young man about to leave looks at Mina first.

Her mother kneels and prays in the ghostly pews long emptied of people. Mina watches Jesus' unmoving lips and waits for her mother's routine to conclude. If I kiss Jesus, Mina wonders, maybe he would reject her tainted lips. Or maybe he would kiss her back as fondly as a father might. He was God's son, so wasn't he capable of anything?

Fourteen is far too old to believe in magic, but tonight she will do anything to appease her mother. She shuffles to the altar, a penitent's walk, and kisses his wooden face. He merely stares, impervious. She tries prayer because her mother says she must pray for forgiveness, but instead her hands keep moving to free the doves trapped in the stained glass. A splinter enters her palm when she runs her hands across the bench smelling of vinegary sawdust.

A man taps her mother's back: the pastor, a man with yellow fingernails and a tenuous mustache, a man who looks unable to help himself. His solemnity is touching, ridiculous.

⤝

Pastor Seo, Mrs. Lim says to the pastor of the Korean service she does not attend, which is conducted before the English one.

You're here again, Mrs. Lim.

He must have meant to comfort them with that practiced smile and certainty that his God has all the answers. But this is what Mina will remember: the waxy candlestick holders. The pastor's smug pity, the way his pin-striped trouser cuffs collect dust. The woman on her knees scrubbing the cold floors. Used to the endless troupe of sinners, she does not look up once.

⤝

Everything is the way it was before except that it is not. Over dinner Mina's mother refuses to talk. Mina longs to hear her mother's comforting songs: Man is the heavens, woman is the earth. Yin and yang. The effete *yangban* with white scholar's hands who rescues the *sijo*-writing *gisaeng* from her courtesan's chambers and then together, live blissfully ever after. America, where rice grows on trees. The predictable lull of her mother's fantasies that neither believes anymore.

Her mother stares into a glass of water and tries to wipe away her reflection with her thumb. Her smile grows shapeless as she says, You're too grown up now, at the age of all loneliness.

Mina feels old and grave; she tries to erase the distress from her mother's face with a kiss, and succeeds for a moment as her mother leans restfully against her.

I have you, Mina says. I know everyone in our neighborhood! I'm never lonely.

Suddenly her mother says, You've become beautiful.

She removes her diamond earrings, her only precious gems, and forces them into her daughter's palms until the brittle edges cut into her skin.

Then Mina knows, something must be wrong. Her mother is gone.

↤

She is the only kind of mother that Mina knows. She is a mother who used to nibble on raw silkworms to keep her skin as pale as pearls, who now prays out loud at night that God make her His wife.

She is a mother who leaves Mina a note the next day saying, You shouldn't behave that way with men. It is twilight, autumn of 1976. Birds from China have migrated and settled on the naked trees surrounding their house. Her mother has not returned. Perhaps she has gone to a church retreat or stayed late at work, though she has not told Mina anything. In the refrigerator, there is a plastic tub of kimchi and fresh produce; a flank of pork has been left out. It will rot, Mina thinks, as she pieces together the evidence, imagining a pink flank and bony rump hooked up at the butcher's, and squeezes herself until it hurts. She drops her schoolbag and withdraws like a hermit crab. If she flees to Hana's home and forgets that her mother is right to punish her, she will be safe. But she has never run away.

When the soybean curd man outside keens his sales song, it is dark. She wraps her mother's sheets around her shoulders like a shroud, and lies on the ground. She has washed and tried to cleanse herself, tried to wipe the memory of Junho's hands and lips from her lips, from her breasts, but there is still Junho on her skin, in her hair, under the crests of her fingernails. Mina will not let the story end this way. Tomorrow she will go to school and act as if she is somehow still the same person. She will look for her mother. But tonight she waits on the cold floor, certain that what is lost will return.

ACKNOWLEDGMENTS

My deepest gratitude goes to my editors, Kathryn Court and Allison Lorentzen at Penguin Group (USA) and Sarah Savitt at Faber and Faber UK. Their creativity, collaborative instinct, and passion for books have made this journey a pleasure. I'm also indebted to the staffs at Viking and Faber and Faber, who have been tireless in their support. My love and thanks to my indefatigable agent, Susan Golomb, whose faith in my work, kindness, and ability to think like a writer have made all the difference.

I want to thank my early teachers and mentors, Stephen Yenser, Ross Shideler, Heather McHugh, Hugh Houghton, Hermione Lee, Tom Jenks, and Carol Edgarian. Without this early support, I would never have dared consider myself a writer. The learning and community in the MFA program at Warren Wilson College were invaluable. In particular, I'm grateful to Peter Turchi, Ellen Bryant Voight, Lan Samantha Chang, Jane Hamilton, Grace Mazur, David Haynes, Victor LaValle, Robin Black, Aneesha Kapur, Robert Rorke, Rachel Howard, Allison

Paige, Katie Bowler, Ross White, Ed Porter, Mark Prudowsky, Matthew Specktor, Bora Reed, and Larissa Amir, and to Abby Wender for her friendship, her incredible poems, and her way of being.

The organizations that support writers gave me resolve and a community. Thank you to the Napa Valley Writers' Conference and the Squaw Valley Community of Writers, and to *Narrative* magazine and *The Kenyon Review* for taking a chance on a new writer.

The manuscript readings by Sunil Rao, Kira Obolensky, Michael David Lukas, Kim Stoker, and early readers Charlie Kang, Chris Causey, Mark Lee, and Peter Kipp helped the writing experience be a little less lonely. Thanks to Heeyoung Kim for her fact checking; David Kim and Katherine Lee for their expertise; Christine Zilka for her friendship and her example; Jenny Whitney, Beth Lee, Colin Cavendish-Jones, Camilla Jorgensen, Margareta Wilhelmsson, and Tiziana Bertinotti for their love and support; Tanya Gibson, my AWP buddy and fellow dreamer; Steve Kim, who has seen me through the entire journey; Shirley Park and her family for their love and help; Heidi Snyder and family, wherever they are; girlfriends Linda Kwon, Suyoon Ko, Sora Kim-Russell, and Tammy Chu, who keep me company in Seoul; Doualy Xaokaothao, who has pulled me through more than once; Jean Lee for sharing her creative energy; Steve Herman, supporter and friend; John Glionna for being unpredictable; and Kyemyeong Lee for keeping me hopeful and sane. My love and respect to my activist friends, and to all my North Korean defector friends who have given me a family.